Dreamcatcher

To Gary, who has always been there
for our children

Dreamcatcher

Jen McVeity

Lothian
BOOKS

Acknowledgements

With gratitude to Pam, my sister—who gave me the
dreamcatcher. Plus my thanks to Bob Warneke of Warneke
Marine Mammal Services for his patience and help with
the whale scenes. I also gratefully acknowledge the
financial support of the Victorian government, Australia,
through the assistance of Arts Victoria.

Thomas C. Lothian Pty Ltd
11 Munro Street, Port Melbourne, Victoria 3207

First published in Australia 1999
Reprinted 1999
First published by Orchard Books, USA, in 1998
as *On Different Shores*

National Library of Australia
Cataloguing-in-Publication data:

McVeity, Jen.
Dreamcatcher.

ISBN 0 85091 964 9.
I. Title.

A823.3

Cover design by Jo Waite Design
Typeset by DOCUPRO
Printed in Australia by Griffin Press Pty Limited,
A division of PMP Communications

Chapter 1

My half sister, Laura, did a slow, soaring back somersault, and I wondered what she thought about as she floated high in the air above us. Did she have dreams of flying? Of winning world titles? Or nightmares about landing with a crash on her head?

'Don't arch your back!' called her coach. She tensed in midair and came down with a twist that nearly sent her flying off the trampoline. So much for soaring. 'You have to get more height,' was all her coach said. 'Try it once again.'

'It looked pretty good to me,' I muttered.

'Yes,' said Kate. Two tiny frown lines creased between her eyes as she watched her daughter. Her worry lines. They deepened every time Laura reached the top of her bounce, arms stretching nearly to the girders of the old gym's roof. God, she went high. At times she could make you forget she was so young. At other times ... I felt my own pair of worry lines start. 'She really does want to be the best,' Kate said.

Kate was Laura's mother and my step-mother. If you can work that out. I suppose you could say she was my second mother, but I never called her that. Years and years ago, when she had married Dad, she had asked me to call her Kate like all her friends did. I guess that's how I've always thought of her.

'Stay in the centre!' Laura was practising one of her special tricks this time — a seat drop into a somersault into another seat drop. She made it look easy. Me, I'd always thought just a seat drop was pretty clever. I'd taught that to her ages ago on the rusty trampolines at the back of the local community centre.

'Watch this!' I'd said. I'd been showing off a bit, going from knee drop to seat drop three times in a row, arms and legs everywhere, and somehow managing to scramble back to my feet at the end.

'Again,' Laura had cried. 'Show me again!' And then: 'Let me try!' She had been so young then I'd had to lift her up onto the tramp. It was probably just a fluke that she figured it out on the first try. And did it better than me. But you could tell she was hooked from that minute on.

Somehow, after that she always managed to talk me into taking her to the community centre most days after school. I hung around with some friends and got overloaded on the free coffee while she latched onto some older kids who taught her things like cradles and back overs and turntables. All the tricks had such weird-sounding names, I didn't know what she was talking about half the time. When winter came and no one was there to teach her, she started making up her own tricks. The seat drop somersault was one of them.

That was the first thing Kate saw when she caught up with us one day at the centre: Laura, twisting and turning high in the air and looking like she was about to land right on her head at terminal velocity. I thought Kate was going to kill me. I mean, I was supposed to be in charge, and I guess that meant keeping Laura safe from muggers and murderers — and presumably from breaking her neck. Hanging around in midair probably didn't exactly classify as safe. But Kate just sort of looked at me and then at Laura laughing and bouncing high out of the somersault — and going straight into about ten other tricks.

'See this,' she cried to Kate. 'It's a three-hundred-and-sixty turntable.' She didn't stop talking even when she was in midair. 'And this is a straddle jump into a stomach drop. And this ...' And Kate had watched, given me a little smile, and then marched Laura straight into the office and enrolled her in trampoline classes.

───

'That's right. Tuck harder! Harder!' Laura was in a roof belt now, ropes strung over the girders high above while the coach watched her doing double back 'saults. 'Work for that height,' he called. Around and around she went. Didn't she ever get dizzy?

Kate pushed back stray bits of hair and looked at her watch. 'They're late,' she said. 'We'll have to hurry. Your dad's home to dinner.'

That was a change. Dad never had time for dinner. As a politician he thought it was his duty to put work first, last, and in the middle. He usually came home to change his shirt and then raced back out to change the world again.

'What's the big occasion?' I asked Kate. 'Doesn't he have a meeting tonight? No speech to make to the young mothers? No ships to launch?'

4

'Tess!' Kate said my name warningly. She looked at her watch again. The coach must have seen her.

'That's all for today,' he told Laura. 'Good work. See you Thursday.' After two hours of slog and sweat, that was all he had to say?

'That was great,' I said.

'Thanks,' said Laura. She was still breathing hard. 'It had better be. The state selection comp is only a couple of weeks away.' Through the close-fitting leotard, you could see little groups of muscles all the way down her rib cage.

'You'll romp it in,' I promised.

'Will you be coming?' she asked. It wasn't as dumb a question as it seemed. During the week I lived with Dad and Kate and shared a bedroom with Laura. But I spent every weekend with my mum at our house on the beach. The competition was on a Saturday, which meant I had to get Mum to drive me back into town to watch.

'I wouldn't miss it for the world,' I told her. Mum would understand.

'What about Dad?' She sort of tossed the question into the air between Kate and me. 'Do you think he'll come too?' On the trampoline, she looked so sure and strong and free. Suddenly she looked as if she was about to cry.

'I know he'll try.' Kate put her arm around

her and gave her a hug. 'He's very proud of you. Very proud of you both,' she added, looking at me. It was typical of Kate to include me in, to always play fair, even though I wasn't her daughter. But this time she was wrong. Dad was proud of Laura; he talked a lot about her trampolining skills. He used to boast about my marks at school, my being the best swimmer, the best debater, the best team captain. But he didn't now. It's been a long time since Dad could find something about me to be proud of anymore.

Chapter 2

'I'm having trouble with my double back somersault,' said Laura. It was roast lamb and rivetting conversation for dinner. Dad was home.

'I see,' he said. 'Pass the potatoes please, Kate.'

'I'm sure you'll get it right soon,' Kate said to Laura.

'Coach says I need more height,' she answered. She hadn't even looked at her food.

'Try and get fitter.' Dad was spooning mint sauce over roast potatoes. 'That will help.'

'I might just make it a single 'sault,' said Laura.

'You can do it,' said Dad. 'You just have to try harder.'

There was silence, if you didn't count the sound of Dad chewing roast lamb and Laura tap, tap, tapping against the side of her plate with her knife. Dad had a way of making silences turn you inside out and upside down. That's what our family dinners were all about now. Silence as he read report cards, silence when you showed him a project from school, silence and nobody moving while he debated how you could have done better, tried harder, reached higher. Once, the silence had stretched for nearly five minutes as he calculated the speed Susie O'Neill, the fastest female swimmer in the world, swam in kilometres per hour. Then he did the same sum for my best swim time. The one I got bronze for in the state championships. No prizes for guessing which number was the best. After he read out the figures, there was the world-famous silence again. Like the silence you'd feel falling down the Grand Canyon. You want to scream, but nothing comes out.

'I think the single 'sault looks fine,' I told Laura. 'Your form's better. It gives the routine more elegance.'

'She'll get the double. She won't quit,' said Dad. He glanced at me. Not like you, he almost seemed to add.

'How's that proposal for the new speed humps going?' Kate interrupted. She was an expert at deflecting World War III at the dinner table.

'I think we have an agreement in principle from the local councils ...' Just mention work and Dad was off. 'Many of their objections are not particularly germane ...' I tuned out round about paragraph three. Once he started talking, Dad tended to go into speech mode, using huge long words like he was sitting in Parliament or something. I used to get a kick out of watching him work the crowds and the media, scoring points with a handshake or a smile. But it was all old hat to me now. Kate was listening, hair neatly back into its bun, head tilted to one side like she was really interested. I wondered if she really was or was just being polite. When she met Dad she was a tutor at the university. Now she was a full-scale lecturer in English literature specialising in the metaphysical poets. Whatever they were. Perhaps she really did understand Dad after all.

'Want to come to Mum's place with me this weekend?' I whispered to Laura. It was summer holidays with all the long, lazy days of freedom stretching ahead. It would be great down at the beach.

'Thanks,' said Laura. 'But I've got training on Sunday.' I knew that. She always did.

'Maybe Mum will drive you. I could ask.'

'And I've got an extra session on Saturday too. With the selection titles so close.'

'Oh.' That put an end to that idea.

'You could stay here,' she said eagerly. 'We could go to a movie Saturday night.'

'Oh, Laura!' I almost wailed the words. 'I can't. You know I can't.'

She nodded, not looking at me. 'Sorry,' she said. She was still pushing food around her plate. She hadn't eaten anything. 'I shouldn't have asked.' But she always did ask. Even as a tiny kid, she had hated it on the weekends when I went to Mum's and she was left to sleep in our bedroom alone. Most toddlers' first words were *Mum* or *more* or *no*. At twelve months, Laura had grabbed hold of my sleeve and said, 'Stay!'

'You know Mum wants me there,' I said. Laura nodded again. We both knew the script by heart now. And besides, I wanted to be with Mum too. Needed to be. It was like a time of rest. 'Mum has been asking me to spend more time with her,' I said. 'Not less.' I hadn't dared to tell Laura that before. She looked up in sudden panic.

'You wouldn't!' she begged. I reached out to ruffle her hair and then pulled a bit of it to make her smile.

'Not without you,' I said, grinning. 'There's only so much peace and quiet I can take.'

'Of course, the noise level is a problem ...' Dad had raised his voice so that Kate could hear him in the kitchen. She was collecting plates, although normally that was Laura's and my job.

'What about the people who live there?' asked Kate. She returned to the table, looked at Laura's untouched meal, and sat down again. 'What are they saying?'

'The general feeling from the constituents' — Dad never called them people, they were all constituents. Potential Persons to vote for him in the next election — 'is really very positive.' I could just see him standing around listening carefully to his constituents, taking notes, nodding gravely. By the time he got home he was usually right out of nods. 'We'll need to monitor the situation closely,' he was saying. 'I might do a quick constituency tour around the end of the month.'

I felt Laura stiffen. 'Not the twenty-seventh,' she said. 'The state selection comps are then. You have to be there!' she cried.

'Of course I'll try,' Dad told her. I'd heard that before.

'He'll try,' I muttered to Laura. 'But don't count on it.'

'Behave yourself, Tess,' said Dad. Kate gave me her warning look and shook her head slightly. 'You don't seem to realise that other people, too, call on my time.'

'Other people always want your time,' I said. 'What about us?'

'Naturally, I want to be with my family

first.' Dad had used that line often in press interviews. I had read it in the local newspaper many times.

'Like you tried for my parent–teacher night?' I asked. Kate had gone to the school alone — as usual. But this time she had sat stunned as all my teachers shook their heads and waffled on through clichés about wasting time and unfulfilled potential. Dad had attended some local council meeting on merging boundaries. As usual.

'I didn't need to talk to your teachers. Your report card said it all!' Dad's voice rose right out of parliamentary mode. Kate put a hand on his arm to quiet him. 'Maybe if it had been different, I would have been there.'

'Like last year?' I cried. Last year on my report card, I had received an A in every single subject. Last year Dad had gone and spoken at a ship launching. The year before that he had been guest speaker at a conference on euthanasia.

'You will come, won't you?' Laura was almost begging now. 'To the trials?' She kicked me under the table to shut me up. Laura always wanted peace at any price.

'Of course I'll be there,' said Dad. And then he went and spoiled it all. 'Naturally, I'll try.'

Chapter 3

The dream always starts differently, so that it sort of sneaks up on me. Sometimes I am lying on the beach, soaking up the sun and growing hot and lazy before I walk down to the water for a dip. Other times I'm already swimming far out from shore, hands cupped, arms stretching forward, my body slicing through the water. But somehow the dream always goes on the same. My legs start to feel tired, my arms weary, and I turn towards land. It's time to swim to shore. To rest. I feel my arms pull against the water. Lift, stretch, pull, just as I've been trained. I lift my head to check. The shore seems no nearer. Lift, stretch, pull. Lift, stretch ... I check again. No nearer, no nearer at all.

You just have to swim harder, I tell myself. Lift, stretch, pull through the water. Everything seems so heavy. Lift, stretch ... Now my chest starts to burn from lack of air. Harder! My arms flop onto the water, thick and numb. I feel the first tuggings of the rip, sucking at me, seaward. Water churns. I am at the mouth of the bay where the breakers rise crashing against the rocks. They are too near — too strong.

I lift my head again, searching the shoreline. 'Dad!' I cry. 'Dad!' He sits on the beach far away, watching.

'You can do it,' he calls. 'I know you can.' He doesn't move.

Lift, heave, flop. Over and over my arms reach above the water. They feel so heavy now, pulling me down. Lift, heave, and flop. Surely they are too heavy to move? I feel the suck of the waves, the rip, the rocks. The burning takes over. The shore grows distant.

'Dad!' I cry again. It is only a whisper. He can't hear me. Each breath is a struggle, gasping for air, swallowing water. My whole body is leaden now, it is too much effort to even float. And the breakers are pulling at me, pounding at me, stronger each time ...

~

The dreamcatcher stopped the rest of the dream. It often did. I jolted awake, panting for breath in the quiet of the bedroom I shared with Laura. Above me, the dreamcatcher hung, a circle, woven in a web of cotton, all in black, so I couldn't see it in the darkness. But I knew it was there. I reached out to feel the feathers hanging from the bottom. They were tattered and worn from the repeated touch of fingers.

Dad had given me the dreamcatcher. Before the silences, before the fights, had come the first bad dream. The night he had been elected to Parliament, he and Kate had come home to find me white and shaking, clutching the baby-sitter, refusing to sleep.

'The waves will get me,' I told them. 'They're pulling me under. In the dream.' Kate had held me and stroked my hair until the trembling stopped. But it had been Dad who carried me back to bed, who sat with me and talked. Dad who rose at last and fetched something from a dusty tin in his study and let me unwrap it from the bed of tissues, yellow with age.

'My father gave me this.' And his voice was quiet when he told me the story. Ancient people believed that in the darkness bad dreams got tangled in the threads and were burned away in the first rays of morning sun.

'And the good dreams?' I was holding on to him, pleading with him to stay.

'And the good dreams ...' He had smiled. 'The good dreams always get through.' And he had taken my hand and held it until I fell at last into a waveless sleep.

Funny how the dreams are still about water. Even now, even though I quit swimming nearly a year ago.

In the darkness, I heard Laura settle and sigh.

'You're still awake, aren't you?' I whispered.

'Yes.' Her voice was as quiet as mine. 'I'm trying to get that double back 'sault right.'

'What?' I sat up in bed and peered across the darkness to her bed. I could just make out a dim outline of her face above the covers. 'You're crazy! How can you practise somer-saults in bed?'

I could almost hear her smile. 'It's easy really. Coach showed us. You just imagine you're doing the trick. Go through each part really carefully in your head, and he says it's almost as good as doing it for real.'

It sounded weird to me. She seemed so young, but already she was playing brain games. I lay back down and stared at the ceiling. It was easier to talk that way.

'Tess?'

'Mmmm?'

'What if I don't get selected? I mean for the titles?' It was hard to believe we were only half sisters. We were so alike. Long ago I had asked the same thing. To myself, of course; I had no one to ask but myself. What if I don't win? What if I'm not fast enough? What if, after all the work and the trying, I wasn't good enough? The night before every swimming competition was filled with 'What ifs' circling, demanding, echoing through my head.

'You'll get selected,' I said. 'They pick two for each age group, don't they?' I knew damn well they did.

'Yes. But if I screw up the selection comp — '

'"But" nothing. You've been ranked number one for your age all year. If you mess it up, they'll figure out a way to get you on the team. They need you there.'

'But what if I bomb out in the state competition? Karen Macoby will be there. She's won three times in a row. And Alison Joseph is putting a double back 'sault with half twist into her voluntary routine.'

And I thought *I* had problems. But how could you tell someone that losing wasn't the end of creation — once you got used to the idea. Laura had spent her whole life training to win. She spent every single bit of her free time at the gym, working on her trampoline routines, doing push-ups, and lifting weights to make herself stronger. She could pull herself up a rope right to the top of the gym without using her legs at all. My stomach muscles ached just to watch her.

'If you don't win,' I said carefully, 'the sun will probably start rising in the west. Clocks will start running backwards and go tock-tick, instead of tick-tock. The whole world will grind to a halt because no one will be able to get to work on time.' That at least got a half laugh.

'Dad would be so disappointed.' She still wasn't convinced.

'Not as disappointed as you, I bet.' Besides, the last time Dad had seen Laura on the trampoline was at the interschool sports competition. And only because he'd been officially invited to present the prizes. Kate was the one who drove her to all the training sessions, who talked with her coach, who put the ointment on her bruises. 'What would Kate say?' I asked.

'I guess Mum would just give me a big hug.' Laura sighed. She was silent. 'She cried once, you know. When I lost one time. Not just because she was disappointed.' Her voice sounded kind of surprised, like she had just discovered something. 'She was crying for me.'

'Well then,' I said. As a clincher in a discussion, it wasn't much. But Laura knew what I meant.

'Tess?'

'Mmmm. Still here.' My eyelids were getting heavy.

'What happened, Tess? When you stopped swimming?'

Halfway through a yawn, I suddenly went stiff. I should have known this was coming again. 'Nothing,' I said casually. 'I just got bored with it, that's all.'

'But you were so good. You had a real chance at the nationals.'

'Yeah, maybe.'

'How could you stop? Just like that?'

I sighed. Why did she always want to know about the swimming? Why? Did she worry that something like that might happen to her in time? I squeezed my eyes and mouth tightly shut at the thought.

'It wasn't any fun anymore.' I had to say something. 'You know, all those laps every day. Up and down a pool. With no one to talk to. You couldn't even have a joke without getting a mouthful of water.' For Laura's sake I tried to make it sound different from her training.

'But it happened so suddenly ...'

'Nah. It had been coming for a long time.' It had too. It was just that I hadn't said anything to anyone. I guess I hadn't realised it myself. It was as if one day I suddenly knew that no matter what I did, no matter how hard I trained, every victory would be kind of flat. As if I could have somehow swum harder, done better every time.

'I don't know how you cope with it. All that training. The competitions ...' I shouldn't have said that. I felt sweat prickle at my neck. I hated to even think that it might happen to her. That she would wake up one morning and discover that winning felt like emptiness. Never enough. I hoped like hell that it would be different for her.

'Tess ...?'

'I just didn't enjoy it anymore.' My voice warned her to leave it alone. I didn't want to go back to that time ever. I could see so clearly still the look on Dad's face when I told him I had quit swimming. He looked as if I had shot him right in the chest and then slapped his face as well. The local papers had picked up the story and kept the articles — and the look on his face — going for weeks. Then the report cards were sent home from school at the end of the year, and the look started up again. And somehow never went away. I had always got top marks. Always. Except for this year. Somehow I managed to fail at least three subjects. And there wasn't an A in sight.

'You were really good, you know,' Laura was still going on. 'You could maybe have beaten Susie O'Neill one day.'

'Sure,' I said. I guess she was still young enough to believe in happy endings. My eyes were stinging from being open so long. It must have been really late. I wondered if Laura would go to sleep, imagining her double back somersaults again.

'Do you know what *Laura* means?' I murmured into the night. 'As a name?' I had looked it up one day in a book from the school library.

'I've never thought about it.' Her voice also sounded sleepy.

'It means victory. It comes from the word *laurel*. They made a wreath of the stuff and crowned the winners with it. Laura the victorious.'

'Really?' She sounded almost happy. 'Do you think Mum and Dad knew that when they named me?'

'I guess they know it now,' I said.

Chapter 4

I've got two mothers and two bedrooms in two houses I can call home. Sometimes, if I wangle it right, I can get two sets of pocket money as well. Particularly when Mum has just apologised twice for having to work on a Saturday.

'No,' said Mum. 'Kate will have paid you already.' Unlike Dad, Kate made sure she never forgot things like changeover nights and training schedules — and pocket money.

Unfortunately for me, Mum knew it too now. 'Please,' I tried again. 'I really, really need the extra money. I don't have a decent T-shirt left.' I tried to spread my hands out, but it was difficult in the space left after Mum and I, three other models, and a huge mirror were squashed together in the tiny changing room. Nearly all the photographers hired the old warehouse for their shoots, claiming the light was always great. But the changing facilities were the pits.

'What about the white one?' Mum was slapping on makeup at a great rate, both hands working at once. She was leaning over the mirror from the side, using the top half. At her feet, another model, Debbie, was using the bottom half to tease more volume into what seemed an endless mass of hair and curls. 'Didn't I just buy you a white T-shirt a few weeks ago?' asked Mum.

'I washed it with my jeans.' I hated admitting it. I was fond of that T-shirt. 'Now it's kind of gray and streaked. Unwearable.'

'The grunge look is still in,' said Mum. 'Wear it.' She thought it was funny.

'God, sorry, sorry. I'm late.' Rhonda came squeezing into the changing room, hair and words flying. Rhonda was the makeup artist. Just as well she was skinny; she wouldn't have fitted in otherwise. 'Who's on first?' she cried.

'Margot,' said Debbie-with-the-hair.

'Oh, terrific!' Rhonda looked at Mum's face and relaxed about 0.02 per cent. 'Thanks. You've started already.' Mum always took her own makeup to photography sessions. She claimed it was safer than using the same makeup as about twenty other models. And it gave her a head start if the makeup person was late. They usually were.

'Just finishing,' Mum said. 'All that's left is the lips.' She picked up the outlining stick.

'Can we go out for dinner tonight?' I asked. 'Thai food?'

'Why don't I cook spaghetti at home,' she said. She was stretching her lips to fill in the rest of the lipstick. Her words were all distorted. 'I've got som sooce in the freezer.'

'All right.' I moved so Rhonda could get at Mum's hair with a battery of brushes and pins.

'Oh god. Look at the time! Oh god!' Rhonda fussed.

'What are we shooting today?' called one of the other models. She was trying to get at a bit of mirror too.

'Still doing summer gear,' Mum told her. 'For Sleek Chic.' Mum had the perfect look for the older, more sophisticated clothing. Most of the big local dress shops used her for their catalogues. She was really elegant — all long legs and perfect matte skin. No one at school could believe she was my mum. 'But she's beautiful!' they'd cry. 'Really lovely!' And then they'd start taking quick, surreptitious looks at me. Unfortunately, I took after Dad.

'We'll use a softer style today,' said Rhonda, busily brushing. 'Pulled back at the top with soft tendrils escaping.'

'Easy on the spray,' said Mum. Rhonda nodded and pinned. Then she stood back and covered us all with a cloud of hair spray.

I retreated hastily to the edge of the changing room. 'How can you use that stuff?' I asked.

Mum pulled a face, but she didn't complain. 'It's our job,' she said. 'Sleek Chic isn't paying us to be comfortable. We're being paid to make their clothes look great.'

'You shouldn't be using that brand,' I told Rhonda. 'They test their products on animals.'

'So?' Rhonda looked blank.

'So, they put all these rabbits in cages and then they spray their eyes with this stuff,' I told her. 'Every day.'

'The lucky ones only get a light dose,' said Debbie. I'd worked on her before.

'What about the others?' asked Rhonda. 'Lift up. Careful now.' She was helping Mum get into a brightly swirled beach dress, holding it wide over her head so as not to mess up the hair.

'They spend their whole life with running, red eyes,' I told her. 'It's horrible.'

'Try the Body Shop brand,' Mum put in.

She could usually be counted on to support my crusades. 'They don't do animal testing. It feels good on the hair too.'

'It's more expensive.' Rhonda didn't like it.

'It's not really.' Good for Debbie.

'Besides, think about your eyes,' I said. It was my clinching argument. 'You use it all the time.' That got to her.

'Margot dear, the client has arrived.' The photographer poked his head around the door. It was all of him that would fit in the room.

'I'm ready,' Mum called. She slipped on the shoes Rhonda was holding, straightened the dress, and glanced in the mirror for a final quick check. The other models immediately grabbed her space. At the door Mum stopped, took a slow breath, then walked with long grace to meet the owner of Sleek Chic.

'Stephen,' she said, shaking his hand. 'How nice to be working with you again.' Suddenly she seemed very cool and businesslike. Somehow she even seemed taller too.

'How does she do that?' I asked Rhonda as we watched from the doorway. She shrugged.

'It's her job,' she said, echoing what Mum had said before. 'She's a professional.' She was right I suppose. Everyone saw modelling as so glamorous, full of bright lights and parties. Kate was always making comments and asking lots of questions about Mum's photo shoots. She didn't believe me when I told her they were mainly hot lights on scorching days, elbows in your face in cramped changing rooms, and boring hours of waiting around. She saw the photos of Mum in all the magazines, and she thought it was all seafood, champagne and charming rich men oozing charisma.

But Mum often called herself a human clothes hanger. She knew exactly what pose to take to make a dress hang smoothly. She worked hard to remember clients' names, to send out bills promptly, to keep up with the latest photographers and their styles. I guess that's why she always got lots of work. Even when she was pregnant with me, she kept right on modelling maternity clothes for the local stores and catalogues. Dad was furious. I bet I'm one of the few kids ever to appear on the front cover of *Cosmopolitan* — even if it was only as a bulge in Mum's stomach.

Chapter 5

'What if this year we tried a tutor,' Mum said. 'You know, someone to help a bit with school.'

'We can't afford it,' I had to call out to her. I was in the laundry trying to wash spaghetti stains out of my T-shirt. Dinner had been well over before I discovered them, and they looked like they were set to stay forever. I wasn't having much luck with my T-shirts lately.

'We could if your father paid half the fees.' Mum came to lean against the door of the laundry. 'You could try it just for the main areas. Like maths and English perhaps.' It was the main areas I had bombed in so badly last year. Mum was really worried about it, although she tried not to let it show. I guess it had come rather suddenly — from first to fail in less than a year.

'A tutor wouldn't help,' I said. 'Save your money.'

'It wouldn't hurt to try.'

'I'll do better this year. I just didn't hand in any work, that's all. The teachers had to fail me.'

'What happened, Tess?' The words seemed to slip out of her mouth. She looked surprised. I guess she had been dying to ask that ever since the reports had arrived. I concentrated on rubbing spaghetti stains. When had everything suddenly started to seem so boring, so pointless? Had I just woken up and decided it wasn't worth it — all the swimming, the studying, the endless striving? That it was useless to try. I couldn't remember.

'I just couldn't concentrate for a while,' I said. 'It'll be better next year.' I hated for Mum to worry.

I hung the dripping T-shirt over the shower and wandered into my room, wondering what to wear. Living in two houses meant you were always packing suitcases and forgetting things. Last weekend it had been shoes. I had lived in a pair of broken-down sandals for two days. The weekend before that, it had been my hair dryer and brush. This time it had better not get too hot; I was out of T-shirts already. I was halfway out of the room when suddenly I saw the empty hook above my bed. My arms wrapped themselves across my chest, squeezing tightly, making me feel sick. This time there was something else I had forgotten. The dream-catcher ...

'Tess?' Mum had followed me to my room just as I was rummaging through my suitcase. Maybe I had packed it after all.

'Mmmm?' I was shaking out clothes, then hanging them quickly in the wardrobe. Three pairs of shoes this time. No shirts.

'Would it help, Tess, if you came here to live?' I looked up at her. 'I mean forever,' she said.

My eyes prickled suddenly, hot and wet. We had talked about it so often lately. Sometimes, lying in bed alone, hearing the sea soothing over the shingle and Mum's music playing softly in the next room, I just wanted to stay with her forever and not go back. It was so calm with Mum, so peaceful. I folded a pale green jumper and put it on the bed.

'Thanks Mum,' I said, but without even knowing it I was already shaking my head. 'It's not that I don't want to. You know that. But ...'

'I know.' She sighed. 'But there's Laura.' She understood.

I nodded. 'She's my sister.' I felt something really fierce and soft well up inside me. I couldn't leave Laura. It wasn't possible. And Laura would never leave Kate — her mum.

She wouldn't leave our dad either. No matter what hours Dad worked, Laura was always there to greet him when he got home. Mostly it was after we had gone to bed. Somehow she had trained herself to hear his car, even when she was asleep, and there she'd be in her pjs and sleep-bagged eyes to greet him as he came through the door. In the mornings, she dogged his footsteps as he went from shaving mirror to breakfast to front door. That was all she got to see of Dad.

At least I had the memories of the early times. Times before Dad became too busy to come to parent–teacher nights, before he was always out of town for competitions and pre-sentation evenings. When I was young, I used to turn the pages of the album where first Mum and then Kate had pasted all the newspaper pictures and articles about Dad. Sometimes I would be in the pictures too. I had looked through the album so frequently it was dog-eared and shabby. It always fell open at my favourite page. A picture in the local paper so big that Kate had had to paste the picture on one page and the article on another. The photo is of Dad smiling and hugging me, still in my wet bathing suit, hair plastered to my head at the state swim titles. 'Proud MP and fast-as-a-fish daughter" said the caption.

Laura never really got a chance to share those kinds of memories. Instead she gets to leaf through newspaper articles about Dad running committees and making sincere-sounding election promises. Michael Robertson's family hardly rates a mention anymore. Instead, it's all 'Robertson Crusades against Rising Costs'; 'Dedicated Robertson Takes On Corruption Case!'; 'Tireless Robertson Works for a Better World.' If there was a cause, then there was a crusade — and there was always Michael Robertson to back it.

'Maybe you could spend more of the holidays here then,' said Mum. 'And Laura too.'

I nodded. In the bottom of the suitcase there was a pile of fluff in one corner, a dollar coin, and a dirty Life Saver. No dreamcatcher. 'I'll ask Dad and Kate,' I said. 'Next week.'

It was getting really late. I didn't want to go to bed.

'Good night,' said Mum. She bent to give me a kiss. 'Laura is very lucky.'

'Lucky?' She didn't make sense.

'To have you,' said Mum. She smoothed my hair, as if I were a tiny child, and sighed. 'I couldn't stay there,' she said.

When she was gone, I turned on the hall light so that it would shine into my bedroom. It didn't help. The waves and the nightmares came all night.

Chapter 6

It was boiling hot on the top of the cliff high above Whale Bay. Hot and exhausting, and the flies had chosen this day to be particularly sticky, crawling over arms and faces and exploring eyes. It was impossible to brush them away because most of the time we were carrying two full buckets of water. Any movement to get rid of flies meant you spilled most of it.

Three years ago, whales had come to Whale Bay. And got stranded. People had travelled from all over the state to look and watch and gawk from the cliff top. They had trampled huge areas of tea-tree and saltbush as they tried to get a better view. They had spread their picnic rugs on pigface, squashing it to death while their kids played tag among the scrub and tore the tea-tree to shreds. There was a path, of course — not that anyone stayed on it. They all wanted to get a better view, a clearer photo of the great dying whales. And bad luck to any stray bits of vegetation that got in the way of their feet.

When they left, the wind moved in and the sun, and nothing seemed to grow there anymore.

'The Cliff Desert' people started to call it, and every time the wind blew or heavy rain came, more of it fell into the sea below. The council made noises; people wrote indignant letters to newspapers; everyone agreed it was a disgrace. Someone had to do something.

In the end, the four of us had, just because it seemed like a good idea. Cautious Colin, Toni Mioni, Jacob-the-Radical and me, all of us sitting around under the trees at school, swapping great plans. Three hundred trees and shrubs to be planted on the cliff top — one for each kid in the school. A few teachers got interested, the school came up with some money, and then came the crunch. Three hundred trees meant days and weeks of backbreaking work as we dug and staked and planted them all.

It had been the last school project I'd launched before time and energy just seemed to fizzle out.

'I've finished my lot,' called Colin. He pushed thick, sand-coloured hair out of his eyes and grinned. Because he was the biggest and strongest of us all, we always gave him the largest section of plants to water. He still managed to finish first.

'Help me with mine,' begged Toni. 'I'm way behind.'

'You got here late,' said Colin. He was teasing her.

'It wasn't my fault.' Toni tipped water on a series of tiny pigface plants. 'I told Mum I was going to visit Paula, and she insisted on dropping me off there.' Toni rolled dark eyes upward, crossing them. She lives about three minutes away in a house near Mum and me but further back from the beach. Paula lived way in near town. 'I had to wait until she had gone,' said Toni. 'And then catch a bus back.'

'At least you made it,' I said. I slapped at a particularly insistent fly. Water slopped everywhere.

'Do you think she suspects something?' Colin asked. He earned his nickname about five times a day.

'Nah.' Toni laughed. 'No more than usual.' Ever since Toni's dad had left them years ago, her mum had always been super careful in looking after Toni and the twins. 'She's just into one of her see-more-of-the-children cycles,' said

Toni. 'She was so busy making eye contact and doing the quality listening thing that she nearly ran over two pedestrians on the way.'

'So what if our parents find out?' asked Jacob. 'Would they really care?' Maybe his parents wouldn't. They were into physics and alternative lifestyles and had built a solar-powered house on one of the highest points in Breaksea. In fact they even knew Jacob was part of a conservation group that met most Sundays trying to lobby for 'cleaner rivers, cleaner air, cleaner seas'. But sometimes I wondered what would happen if they connected 'Jacob's little group' with the Green Guerrillas who had reported the local paint factory for pouring poisonous waste into the river or who had carefully painted 'Get Drastic about Plastic' for three weeks in a row on the huge glass doors of the local shopping mall.

'Green Gang Strikes Again!' had been the small headline on page three of last week's local paper. After that, we decided it was too risky to keep on with the painting job. We had run out of paint anyway. The paper reckoned that we were a gang of 'at least twenty hard-core conservationists'. In actual fact, there were only the four of us, meeting here on the cliff top, lugging buckets of water and trying to keep the flies and the sweat out of our eyes.

'If my parents ever found out, they would have a fit,' said Colin. His folks thought he went to a friend's place every Sunday to learn guitar. They hadn't figured out yet that he could still only play 'The House of the Rising Sun' with a three-finger strum.

'My mum would too,' agreed Toni. She and Colin had finished her section now and had moved on to help Jacob. Colin wasn't even out of breath.

'They might think it a good thing,' said Jacob. 'After all, at least we're trying to do something useful.' Sometimes I think he liked the idea of being a martyr.

'Mum would hit the roof,' Toni said positively.

I wondered what would happen if any of my family found out about the Green Guerrillas. And that I was the leader. Maybe Mum would think it okay, once she got used to the idea. And maybe Kate would come down in my favour after she had weighed up all sides in her careful way. She was like that. But Dad ... Mention anything even vaguely illegal and Michael Robertson the Crusader instantly turned into Michael Robertson, Extremely Proper Parent and Politician. You could forget about the roof.

You'd hear him ranting about 'appearances' and 'responsibility' and 'reputation' until the whole lid came off the world.

'Let's just keep our mouths shut!' I snapped and then immediately wished I hadn't. Toni looked at me curiously and Jacob frowned. I rubbed my eyes. They felt as if they had a whole beachful of sand in them. I hadn't had enough sleep by a long shot. And without the dreamcatcher tonight would be just as bad. 'How's the pharmacy campaign going?' I said, changing the subject.

Jacob coughed and looked embarrassed. 'There was a bit of a backfire there,' he said. We waited, but he didn't go on.

'What happened?' asked Colin at last. 'Did they nearly catch you or something?'

'Er ... it was the posters,' said Jacob. He shrugged, then turned the tap to fill a bucket and watched it carefully. The posters had been designed by Jacob to stop people from buying cosmetics made by companies that use animals to test their products. They showed a picture of a rabbit like the ones I told Rhonda about with its eyes full of pus and gunk. It looked really dreadful. Underneath was a list of all the cosmetic companies that use animals for testing. We had taped the posters on the outside of pharmacy windows on Saturday after they closed for the weekend. On a few shops, if we were lucky, they would stay there all weekend. Jacob was still watching water.

'Well?' demanded Colin. 'The posters. What about them?'

With a sigh Jacob turned off the tap and pulled a folded poster out of his pocket. All of us stopped lugging water and watched. 'I was so careful to get the spelling of the companies' names right,' he said. He slowly went on unfolding. 'But somehow ... I forgot to check the rest.' He stretched out the poster with another shrug. There was the picture of the poor rabbit. There was the list of companies neatly written in columns. And on top was the heading, written in huge capitals: DON'T TORTOURE ANIMALS! Someone had drawn a huge circle around the misspelling and had scrawled underneath DON'T TORTURE THE ENGLISH LANGUAGE! in letters almost as big.

'Oh my god,' said Toni and started to laugh. 'I put up three of them last week. I never even noticed!' I'd put up two myself. And had been too busy fumbling with sticky tape and ducking out of sight of curious window-shoppers to even read the words. I shook my head, trying not to smile. Jacob had put so much time into those posters.

'Oh, well,' I said. 'They say even bad publicity is good publicity.'

'I suppose at least it means people are reading our stuff,' said Jacob. He gave another shrug and then the tiny beginning of a smile.

'But they'll know now we're kids,' said Colin suddenly. 'That gives us away for sure.' He looked around, as if he expected to see some spy who had trekked over five hundred metres of sand dunes to catch us in the act.

'Relax,' said Toni. 'Maybe they'll think we're a bunch of dissatisfied maths teachers. Everyone knows they can't spell.'

'Or a bunch of terrorists from overseas. 'We haf a bomb. Stop spoilin' the oceen or we blowe yoo up," said Jacob. He was laughing now.

It was nearly a dead heat to see who finished watering first. Toni, Jacob and Colin won by half a bucket. I dribbled the rest of my water onto a few struggling bits of saltbush and joined them under the only tea-tree that was big enough to offer shade. The ground underneath the tree was completely flattened from all the times we had sat and talked there.

'How's the Comcor campaign going?' I asked Colin.

'Comcor?' asked Jacob. 'Which one is that?'

'The smokestack,' Colin reminded him.

There were a lot of local companies on our hit list. Comcor was a huge, into-everything company that employed about a thousand people in our area. It was also the main sponsor of the local football team, which nearly took out the grand final last year. Everyone was so busy knitting football scarves in the right colours they never even noticed the tonne of dust and smoke pouring out every day from the huge chimney the company had built on the outskirts of town. It smoked all day and night. And it stank.

'The usual silence from the minister,' said Colin. 'I've sent three letters to his office now, and still no reply.' Colin wrote regularly to the minister for the environment. His friends from all over the country mailed the letters, so it wouldn't look as if they came from the same place. And person.

'What about Comcor?' asked Toni. 'What did the big chiefs say?'

'The same old "we have the best interests of the community at heart".' Colin picked up a couple of stray pipi shells and rubbed them together. 'But they never say what's coming out of the chimney.'

'Give them one more try,' I said. 'Or can you think of a better way?'

'Not yet,' said Colin. 'Work on it, will you.'

He grinned at me. That was what I was good at. Scheming. Coming up with the action ideas.

'That's it, then. Anything else?' My back was killing me. It was time to close the meeting. Excuses about friends and guitar lessons could only be stretched so far. 'Everyone right for Tuesday night?'

On Tuesday night one of the biggest fashion houses around, Elle-Louise, was having a fashion show. Some of the swimsuits to be modelled were made out of seal fur. Mum had accidently mentioned it to me. On Tuesday night, Colin's parents thought he was going bowling, and Jacob's folks thought he was playing on a computer at a friend's place. Toni was supposedly going to the movies with me. But Tuesday night, Colin would turn into a sealer, while the rest of us would be wearing white costumes and home-made masks with the huge brown eyes and soft fur of a seal pup's face. Outside the entrance to the fashion show, newspaper photographers would be waiting, and maybe even a news team from our local TV station. They would have been tipped off by an anonymous phone call I would make early Tuesday morning. One thing Dad had taught me well was the importance of the right publicity.

Tuesday night, just as the mayor and all the

most important dignitaries arrived, we would march out to meet them in our costumes. And show them what it was like to be present at a seal slaughter. We'd all be carrying placards condemning the use of animal fur in clothing. 'Swim in your own skin — not mine!' was the slogan for the night.

I just hope we got the spelling right.

Chapter 7

'Tighten that rotation. That's it. Tuck harder! Tuck!' It was a repeat performance like hundreds of others.

Sunday, five P.M., was changeover time. Mum always drives me to the gym where Laura trains. It's closer than Kate and Dad's house. Neutral territory.

Everyone was in their usual positions. The coach was calling instructions by the trampoline, Laura was in the air above him, and Kate was watching at the back, worry frown in place. You could almost see her making notes in her head, earnest and methodical.

'Hello,' she said to us. 'Much traffic on the road?'

'Not much,' said Mum. 'A bit hot though.' It was always like this, the two of them making polite conversation, as if they were strangers meeting for the first time. I once figured out they had known each other for over a decade, meeting Friday afternoons and Sundays, when I did the changeover. Over a thousand meetings and they still talked about the weather.

'You've been getting lots of work, I see.' Kate was smoothing her hair, fidgeting with her shirt collar. 'You're in the Myer catalogue again this week.' She always fussed about what to wear and put on extra makeup on changeover days. As if Mum would notice.

'Yes, it's been busy. How are you enjoying your vacation?' The universities were closed of course for the summer. Lucky Kate.

'It's been lovely.' Polite questions. Polite answers.

'You must have had a good weekend,' Kate said to me. 'You look exhausted!'

'Sure,' I said. If you call lugging hundreds of buckets of water after getting about two minutes of sleep a night good fun. But being with Mum was always nice. Restful somehow.

'Oh, Kate.' Mum was flicking through her handbag, acting really casual. 'I nearly forgot your book.' She finally produced an Elizabeth Jolley novel Kate had lent her weeks ago. Once, in an effort to make conversation, Mum had mentioned how she admired the current Australian writers. She meant writers like Jennifer

Rowe and Kerry Greenwood who did all the mystery stories. That's all she ever reads. But Kate had leapt at the chance to keep Mum supplied with a steady supply of highbrow works ever since. Mum had never told her the truth. Too embarrassed, I guess. 'Thanks very much,' she told Kate, handing the book over. I wondered if she had actually read it.

'Did you enjoy it?' asked Kate.

'Elizabeth Jolley is a very fine writer,' said Mum. She hadn't read it.

'Good! Good!' said Laura's coach in the background. 'That's all for today.' He came over to join us.

'That's a very impressive routine you've worked out for Laura,' said Mum.

'She's a very impressive girl,' he said. He liked Mum.

'Is she going to do the single or the double somersault?' Mum had heard all about it from me. 'For the selection trials?'

'We'll see how she goes nearer the time,' he said. 'Laura will make her own decision.' That's what he thought. He didn't know about Dad.

'I'll do the double.' Laura was putting on her shoes. Her voice came out fiercely, as if daring us to say different.

'We'll see,' said the coach. 'Plenty of time yet.'

'Have you got everything?' Kate called to her.

Laura was gathering armfuls of drink bottles, towels, and sports bags. I grabbed some of the stuff left on the floor.

'What's for dinner?' Laura asked. 'I'm starving.'

'Special treat tonight,' said Kate. 'Spaghetti bolognese.'

I stifled a sigh. Spag bolognese twice in three days. Not good. Long, long ago I used to dream about Mum and Kate becoming best friends. Somehow I always thought they would have had a lot in common. Apart from both wanting to marry Dad, of course. Now all I wished was that they'd move on just a fraction from talking about the weather onto the next stage. Like what they were planning for dinner.

'And there's rhubarb pie for dessert,' added Kate. 'Gloria's coming to dinner.'

'Oh no!' Laura and I both cried.

'Why?' I asked, but I didn't expect a reply. Gloria was Dad's mother, and she came to dinner for one reason only. To check up on us. To check that Kate was doing her duty as the ideal mother, that Laura and I were being the perfect children, that her darling son, Michael, was being the most wonderful politician in the world. Gloria had a way of making even a simple question like 'How is your holiday?' sound like the Inquisition.

I looked quickly across to Mum. Maybe I could go home with her again. Stay an extra day or two. But Mum was looking at Kate. Did I just imagine it or did they give each other a look, half sympathy and half resignation. Did Mum's eyelid really close in a tiny wink?

Laura was too busy groaning to notice. 'Not Gloria!' she protested.

'Come on,' said Kate. 'You can help make the pie.'

'Why don't you make almond pudding instead?' Laura asked, sounding hopeful. 'Then she won't taste the cyanide.' Kate tried to look shocked, but her lips twitched. Maybe she'd had the same idea.

'See you soon.' Mum gave me a hug and whispered softly into my hair, 'I love you', like she always did. Then she was nodding goodbye to the coach, giving Laura a hug too, and smiling carefully at Kate.

'See you on Friday?' she asked. Changeover times were always the same. But they checked with each other every time.

'Six o'clock.' Kate nodded. 'We'll be there.'

'Have a good week,' Mum called to us all.

'Drive safely,' answered Kate.

Polite farewells too.

Chapter 8

'Very nice pie, Kate.' Gloria was daintily dabbing her lips with a napkin. 'Although I would have made the pastry a little crisper.'

'Actually, Laura made it,' said Kate.

That was different. Laura could do no wrong. 'Lovely, dear.' She beamed. 'Aren't you clever?'

'Thank you.' Laura had politeness down to a fine art.

'And what have you been doing?' My turn now. I didn't get the same smile. After all, I was Margot's daughter — the one who walked out on her darling son. 'You look exhausted.' She made it sound like a crime.

'Watering the plants. Up the top of Whale Bay.'

'Where is that?'

'You know,' said Kate. 'The revegetation

project that Tess did with the school.' Gloria had actually been there while the school principal ignored the pouring rain and told a lot of wet and dripping people how dedicated and entrepreneurial we all were. Colin and Jacob, Toni and I had stood there with proud, silly grins on our faces, getting drenched. Dad had been away somewhere of course. Gloria had hunched under the lion's share of Kate's umbrella, watching with a look on her face, as if the rain and her ruined shoes were all my fault.

That was the last time it had rained for months. Half the plants had nearly died ten days later in a sudden heat wave. Our meeting there every Sunday to pour buckets of water over them had been the start of the Green Guerrillas.

'Of course, I remember now.' Gloria nodded at me. 'Your little garden project, Tess.' Three hundred plants over seven hundred square metres was a damn sight bigger than her backyard. But everyone else's projects were little to Gloria.

'Why is it called Whale Bay?' asked Laura. I'd forgotten she wouldn't know. She came to Mum's place so rarely.

'There was a mass stranding,' I said. 'Over

thirty whales beached themselves on the shore. No one knows why.' We had been away at the time, in Queensland on holiday. I was glad I hadn't seen them. I had heard though. While Mum and I had been shopping and catching up on movies and laughing our heads off on the roller coaster in Dreamworld, the great whales had been dying slowly and horribly on the beach. I paused, blocking newspaper images from my imagination.

'What happened?' asked Laura. 'Did the whales get away?'

'They got three back into the water,' I said reluctantly. 'The rest were too far gone, or too heavy to move.' Their skin had cracked and blistered while the sun beat down on them and slowly baked the giant bodies to death. Seagulls had swarmed by the thousands and pecked at the loosening skin and eyes. I couldn't bear to think about it.

'I heard you couldn't go down to the bay for months afterwards,' Kate said. 'Because of the smell.'

'Really, Kate!' Gloria looked revolted. 'Not at the dinner table. Please!'

'What did you think about my latest election speech?' Dad asked her. 'I thought my stand against the commercialisation of national parks was particularly well received.'

'Yes, it went quite well.' Gloria pursed her lips. We all waited. Then it came. 'But' — it was her favourite word — 'the environment has been done to death. I've told you that.'

'Still, it's an important — '

'I thought you could have given more emphasis to child-care funding.' Gloria acted as if he hadn't spoken. 'The family is very big this year.'

'Perhaps I might use that in the Rotary speech I make next week.' Dad carefully straightened his spoon on the empty plate in front of him.

'I was surprised you weren't at the speech.' Gloria shot a stare across the table to Kate. 'After all, you are on vacation.'

Kate had long since given up going with Dad to all his meetings. 'I had to prepare a new course for next year,' she said. 'It's my own idea. Satire and parody. The outline was due last week ...'

'Mmmm.' Gloria began rummaging in her bag. She had a habit of asking questions and then not listening to the answers. 'Here we are now, presents for you children.' She handed over two identical parcels. Kate got up, lips tight, and started clattering plates together fast to clear the table. She headed for the kitchen, not saying a word.

'Thank you.' Laura began to pick at the sticky tape, carefully unwrapping the paper so it didn't tear. I didn't bother. The parcels were the same shape. Gloria could win prizes for picking the most useless presents possible. I dreaded Christmas. When I was three she gave me one of those intricate mechanical sets, the sort that teenagers love. I swallowed half the pieces and was just choking on the largest remnant when Mum found me. Last year she gave me a Barbie doll, all legs and lingerie. I grew out of Barbies a decade ago.

'Aren't you going to open yours?' Gloria was watching me.

'Sure.' I ripped open the package and stared at the bit of garishly painted green and yellow metal inside.

'How unusual!' Laura managed to put both surprise and pleasure into her voice. The minute she stops trampolining, she should turn professional as an actress.

'What is it?' Dad asked. That's just what I wanted to know.

'It's a hook. You put it on the back of the door for your dressing gown.' Gloria smiled archly. No one bothered to tell her we didn't use dressing gowns — she might have bought us some. Fluffy pink with flowers.

Dad gave me a meaningful stare across the table and jerked his eyes in the direction of Gloria. I looked down at the twisted flower hook. The paint was already peeling off in places.

'Thanks.' I managed to get the word out. No academy award for me.

'Anyone for coffee?' Kate had come back from the kitchen.

'I never touch the stuff. You know that,' said Gloria.

'Not for me,' said Dad, shaking his head. He usually swilled it down.

'Did you see Margot's pictures this week?' asked Laura. Her face lit up. 'She looked fabulous!' Mum had done a shoot for High Flyer Fashion. It had appeared over five pages in a popular women's magazine. When I came in to set the table, Laura and Kate had been poring over it as they cooked dinner. Kate had her earnest look on, studying picture after picture of Mum, as if she were learning something new.

'No, I didn't,' said Gloria firmly. She turned to me. 'And how is ... er, your mother?' She never called Mum by her name.

'Fine thanks.'

'I'll just give Mum a hand in the kitchen.' Laura beat me to our escape excuse by milli-seconds.

'I'll come too.' I stood up quickly. 'There are lots of dishes tonight.' Usually we fought over whose night it was not to do the dishes. Gloria didn't seem to notice. She was settling in, happy to give all her attention to Dad.

'The reporting in the *Advertiser* has not been at all accurate,' she began. Laura and I were dead heating it to the door.

'... reporters ... write their own way ...' Suddenly Dad was talking so low it was almost a mumble. The door swung shut.

'Nonsense. You can't let them get away with it.' Gloria's voice still came through clearly. 'It's time you took a stand.'

In the dining room, Dad was saying some-thing, his usual orator's voice low and indistinct. It would go on like this all night. Mumble, mumble, and then Gloria's voice cutting across, high and clear each time.

'Now, Michael! You know I'm right. Really!'

There was only one person in Gloria's world who was completely right. And that was Gloria.

Sometimes I almost felt sorry for Dad.

Chapter 9

At the entrance to Hobbs's Restaurant people were looking at us strangely, if only because we were wearing coats on a summer night. A hot summer night. Underneath the coats, we all wore our costumes; the masks were ready, stuffed in our pockets. Sweat poured down our faces. I could feel great drops of it trickling under my armpits and soaking into the material below.

'It's her!' whispered Jacob. 'The mayor!' It was about the third time he'd said it. A car, low and sleek, was pulling to a stop. I felt myself go rigid, fingers reaching for the mask.

'Hold it!' Colin grabbed at my arm. 'It's only some fat tycoon and his wife.' The couple eased out of their car, all flab and fake smiles.

'Can't imagine her in a bikini,' snorted Toni. 'It would take a whole seal colony to cover her backside.'

'Are the reporters still there?' Jacob craned his neck to look. It was about the third time he'd asked that too.

'Over there.' I pointed again. Dressed in cotton T-shirts and holding cameras, they were easy to recognise. For once, they looked alert and eager. Usually they had to make do with a picture of the local cricket hero for the front page. On the phone that morning, in a disguised voice that kept making me cough, I had promised them a massacre at the mayor's feet. Of seal pups. Even the hardened local TV station had sounded interested. 'They wouldn't miss this for the world,' I said.

'Here's another car,' Colin hissed. We all stiffened. A black Mercedes pulled up, and a swanky-looking couple got out and strolled up the red carpet leading to Hobbs's front door. The man kept stroking his hair. The woman wore more diamonds than clothing.

'No one important,' Toni said.

'They thought they were,' said Colin. Sweat was running down the edges of his face. He kept wiping away the beads on his top lip. The waiting was always the worst part.

'How's the supermarket campaign going?' I asked. 'Anyone need more photocopies?'

Any time one of us went to the supermarket,

we took five or six different photocopies with us and a roll of sticky tape. When no one was watching, carefully selected products were taped with signs. 'Are you eating tuna — or dolphin???' was one favourite we put over the tins of tuna made by companies that still used driftnet fishing methods. 'White paper = Black rivers' was another sign, which we put on toilet paper and kitchen towels that were bleached with chlorine. We had been doing it for three months now. Of course, the supermarket managers kept tearing the signs down. But we had heard that the random nature of the campaign was driving them mad. They had to go around checking the shelves every day, sometimes every hour. The signs were random because it all depended on when any of us could get to the supermarkets.

'I need some more of the "Go Green Clean",' said Jacob. 'For the detergents.'

'Okay. Anyone else?' They all shook their heads. Dad's secretary let me do the photocopying at his office for nothing. She thought it was for school assignments. If she wondered why I was doing assignments in the middle of summer holidays, she didn't ask questions.

'Do we have to keep doing it?' asked Colin. 'It's hardly working. The supermarkets near us are still stocking all the brands we targeted.'

'Don't stop now!' I wanted to shake him. 'We knew it would take ages. That was the scheme. We agreed on six months, we've got to keep at it!'

'It's working,' said Toni more calmly. 'Our local place is hardly selling any of the non-dolphin-safe tuna. I marked all the tins last month. Most are still there.'

'The supermarkets will crack soon,' I said. 'They've got to!'

'Are you sure the reporters are still there?' Jacob craned his neck around the corner to see. The people milling around the doorway to Hobbs's looked at him curiously.

'Watch out!' Colin dragged him back. 'We want the story to be on seal slaughtering — not on "Green Guerrillas Unmasked"!'

'It would make a good story too.' Jacob shrugged.

'Not if we get arrested!' said Toni.

'Sometimes you have to suffer for your ideals.' Jacob was off into his high moral mode again.

'You suffer if you like,' said Colin. 'But leave me out of it. They could put us in jail.' He wiped sweat at the thought. I felt myself go hot and cold together. The things we had done before had seemed small, a bit of a hassle here and there. Nothing really harmful. Suddenly we were into bigger stuff now. I hadn't thought of jail. Cold cells and shouting police and my father's face looking slapped and furious once again.

'Forget the martyr bit,' I said flatly. 'Let's just be smart and stay in operation. And stick to the escape plan like we agreed.' I had planned the getaway route down to the last inch. We would strip off the costumes behind the big dumpster two streets away and then split up and stroll innocently through the streets to home. I would go back for the coats later on.

'They wouldn't put us in jail, would they?' Toni seemed whiter than ever.

'There's nothing illegal about demonstrating.' I hoped I was right.

'That's her! She's here!' cried Jacob. My heart leapt and jerked. Suddenly we were all fumbling with masks and coats and costumes.

'Hurry!' Colin ripped off his coat. Buttons flew everywhere. 'She's getting out of the car!'

'Where's the placard?' I searched frantically.

'Have you got the sauce?'

'My flippers! Where are my flippers?!'

'Come on!' I shouted. The mayor was already halfway up the red carpet. We rushed towards her from the other end, pushing past people.

'Save our seals,' Colin's voice called in a croak, and we all took up the chant.

'Save our seals! Save our seals!'

We marched right up to the mayor, and I pushed the placard into the hands of someone next to her. 'Swim in your own skin — not mine!' it announced. The guy didn't know what to do with it, so he just stood there holding it and looking confused while Toni, Jacob, and I slapped on some flippers and began flopping around in front of everyone like seals on a rock.

'Orrh, orrh.' We did our imitation seal call. 'Orrh.'

'What's happening?' people were calling in return. 'What is it?!'

'Look out!' someone cried as Colin moved in from the side. He was dressed in the dark clothes of a sealer. His mask leered in a cruel grin. In his right hand he held a baseball bat as a club.

'What do we have here?' he cried. 'Seals. Lovely furry little seals!' He marched up to Toni.

'Orrh,' she said in seal-speak. She looked up at him, the big brown eyes of the seal mask pleading with him.

'You'll make a lovely bit of fur coat,' he shouted — and he swung his club hard. We had practised this part for hours. The bat bounced hard off the ground near her head. At the same time he squirted her with tomato sauce from the bottle held up the sleeve of his left hand. *Thud!* He swung the club again.

'Eeeeeeh!' Toni's voice shrieked, high-pitched and piercing. 'Eeeeeeh!' The bat swung again with a thump, and her head fell sideways at a horrible angle. Then suddenly she sprawled forwards into the red sauce and lay deathly still.

A dazzling light suddenly switched on, spot-lighting us all. The local TV crew had gone into action. Jacob and I rocked and swayed, calling loudly. Colin moved on.

'Another one!' he shouted, towering over Jacob. 'Take that!' he cried as he swung the club. 'And that!' The tomato sauce spurted. Jacob's voice rose to a shriek.

'Nooorrrh!' he cried. He tried to escape, dragging himself across the carpet, towards the feet of the watchers. Colin moved faster.

'Look out!' People gasped, moving backwards in horror.

'Orrrrrh!' The bat swung a third time, and then Jacob, too, lay still.

'And now for you!' Colin was laughing mani-acally. He raced over to me as I lay, calling and cowering on the carpet.

'Orrh,' I said, hopefully. The brown liquid eyes in the mask begged for mercy.

'A nice bit of bikini you'll make,' he said. And then the baseball bat came down and more tomato sauce squirted. *Thud*. The bat raised high and swung again. Sauce covered my hair and ran into my eyes, half blinding me.

'Pleeaasssee!' I was wailing. 'Nooooooo!' Real panic seemed to flow into my voice. Colin loomed high above, the bat raised for the final time.

'Stop him!' someone was crying in the crowd. 'Stop!'

'A club for a cub,' shouted Colin. And the bat came swinging down at full force right in line with my head.

We had planned it exactly. Inches away from contact, he stopped. Flash bulbs popped everywhere. We held the tableau for long seconds as the photographers recorded it all. It felt like forever.

'Come on,' called Colin, suddenly cracking. 'Let's go!' With the flashbulbs still blinding us, we broke and ran for the street.

Next morning it was front-page news. Just like we planned. Dad, the master of the media, would have been proud of me. Ha ha.

Chapter 10

Every month or so, Dad rounds us up and takes us to one of his political parties like some kind of happy family on TV — all newly washed hair and smiles. Thursday night it was the Rotary AGM. Dad was giving a speech on the importance of the family in our community. Kate, Laura, and I were taken along as Exhibit A.

It wasn't too bad for the first hour or three. All the local councillors seemed to take turns making sure Laura and I got enough to eat. I even managed to get a glass of champagne off the circulating tray when the waiter wasn't looking. Ladies hovered around, asking polite questions about school and hobbies and friends. You could tell the ones who hadn't kept up with the latest gossip. They still asked me about swimming, and then went silent and mumbled a lot when they found out I had quit ages ago.

A photographer was in attendance — one usually was. Several times Dad came up and put his arm around us, and we all smiled as the flash went off. Even me. I was thinking that this was the second time I would be in the local paper that week. The other Green Guerrillas would enjoy the joke.

By the end of the evening, most of the adults were gathered in close huddles, waving wine glasses around and talking business secrets. Kate was doing her duty as the politician's wife, listening to other people's problems with her serious look and smile and hair all in place. And Dad was circulating and talking, talking and circulating, endlessly nodding. Laura and I ended up in a corner, curled up in a couple of hard chairs, fighting sleep. Kate finally discovered us there and scooped us all out the door to home.

The murmur of the car was like waves, lulling, pulling. '... incredible honour ...' Dad's voice came from far away. '... Council of the Australian Governments ... vital I be there.' I tried to lift my arms. They were heavy, almost paralysed. Far too heavy to swim across the waves.

'... vital you be here too ...' Kate's voice now, low and distant. The waves were growing stronger, tugging incessantly. I felt myself going under, down, down into the old familiar nightmare. 'You'll miss Laura's selection trials ...' My arms jerked wildly. I sat upright in the car, suddenly awake.

'You can't miss her trials.' I leaned over the front seats, hissing the words into the darkness between Dad and Kate. Laura was slumped asleep in the opposite corner of the car. I kept my voice really low. 'You promised her!'

'I promised the premier I'd help too,' said Dad. His voice was short. 'His operation has suddenly become urgent. I'm to go in his place to Canberra next week.'

'Tell them to ask someone else!'

'Don't be naive, Tess.' Dad frowned into the oncoming stream of headlights. 'This is the opportunity of a lifetime! Besides,' — his shoulders moved carefully — 'the Party doesn't ask you to go. They *tell* you to go. Or you can kiss your whole career goodbye.'

'Can you get back Saturday?' asked Kate. 'Take an early plane. The trials don't begin until ten A.M.'

'I'll give it a try,' said Dad. That word again.

'Can't you do better than that?' My voice suddenly rose.

'Don't get melodramatic, Tess.' Dad's voice rose too. He ran a yellow light and turned left sharply. I checked Laura again. In the sudden glimmer of a streetlight, tears were rolling down her cheeks from beneath closed eyelids.

'You can stop pretending to be asleep,' I said loudly. Her eyes opened, and with a blink she sat up. A couple of tears fell forward onto her dress.

'I'm doing the double 'sault, Dad,' she said quietly.

'Good.' Dad's voice was hearty. 'I knew you could do it. You don't need me there.'

'You never intended to come, did you, Dad?' She was almost whispering.

'Nonsense.' He was angry with her now. 'Do you think I arranged for the premier to get sick just to avoid your meet?'

'You said you would come!'

'I'll be there!' Dad's voice had hit about force nine on the Richter scale. 'Kate, what's got into this family?' He meant: speak up, back me up, like you always do.

In silhouette, I watched Kate tilt her head, considering, weighing up sides in her usual way. And saying nothing.

'You're never there,' I said. The words were meant to come out calmly. But somehow my voice lost control. 'You never have been. You never will!'

'This is ridiculous!' Dad thumped both hands against the steering wheel. Abruptly he pulled off to the side of the road and switched off the engine.

'Is it?!' The sudden silence made my voice sound unbearably loud. "I always put my family first" — isn't that what you always say? Well, prove it. Prove it now!'

'It's the Council of the Australian Governments!' Dad was shouting in return. 'The most important conference of the entire year. And I have been asked to go! Don't you understand that?!'

'I don't have to understand anything!' I yelled. 'I can go and live with Mum for the rest of my life! It's Laura you have to make understand!'

'You can't leave home, my girl!' There was outrage in Dad's voice. 'The courts gave me custody five days a week.'

'Don't count on it!'

A cold hand, stiff and small, touched mine. Laura. 'You don't mean that, do you, Tess?' she whispered. I shut my eyes, blocking out her face.

'What's there to stay for?' I said. I turned my head and looked at Kate, shrugging in apology. Why was it so hard to breathe? 'You can come and stay with me for a change,' I said to Laura. 'On the weekends.'

'You're staying with us,' said Dad flatly. 'And that's the end of it.' His voice was loud, final. He turned the key and started the engine again. 'And I'll be at your competition, Laura.' He tossed the words over his shoulder.

The car pulled out abruptly onto the road. I felt Laura's fingers curve hard and biting against mine.

'God, I work myself to a shadow, just for this family,' Dad muttered. His knuckles were white against the steering wheel. 'And this is all the thanks I get!'

'I'm sure you won't disappoint Laura.' In the silence of the car the words came out flat and hard — like a warning. Was it really Kate who'd spoken? It wasn't her usual voice.

'I don't care if you come,' said Laura. 'It doesn't matter anymore.' Her voice sounded strange too. In the darkness I wondered if I was hallucinating. I had heard those words so often, so long ago. When? Where? And then, at last, I remembered. They had once been mine.

Chapter 11

The story and pictures of our seal slaughter had taken over the entire front page of the weekly paper. There was a huge picture of Colin looking absolutely menacing about to crash the bat down on the head of an innocent seal pup — namely me. Luckily, no one would have recognised either of us because of our costumes. I had snuck out and rescued the picture from the recycle pile and cut out the whole story. The paper had certainly done us proud. A two-column article alongside the picture with 'Green Group Takes On Fashion Industry!' in a huge headline. I pasted it into the secret album I kept on the Green Guerrillas. It was getting quite a lot in it now. Dad didn't know it, but he wasn't the only one in the news.

'It looks great!' Jacob had barely waited to hear my voice on the phone before he started talking at the top end of the excitement range.

'The newspaper?' I asked. I tried to keep my voice low — Mum was in the next room doing the ironing.

'Of course!' he cried. 'I went out and got three copies of it!' Obviously his parents weren't home, because he probably could be heard in any room in the house. 'This, on top of the TV segment, is unbelievable!'

Jacob, Colin, and I had been stars for all of thirty seconds on the Wednesday morning news. Unfortunately, Kate had walked into the room just when it came on. I'd nearly died. I'd leaped out of my seat and been so busy trying to block her sight of the TV and get her out of the room that I'd hardly seen a thing. Just a couple of glimpses of Colin crashing the bat down near Jacob's head and tomato sauce looking really gruesome and lifelike spraying everywhere. And then the final, terrible scene, where Colin aimed the bat right at my head with a laugh and an insane look all over his face. I felt quite sick to see it.

I'd never dreamt it would all be so successful.

'Did you see that we have now grown in size?' asked Jacob. "The Green Guerrillas are a well-organised band of over forty youths. Possibly university students ..."'" He was quoting from the newspaper. I laughed.

'We'll be a gang of hundreds next. And going international!'

'Step aside, Greenpeace! Nothing can stop us now!'

'Er ... right.' I wasn't sure we were ready for that just yet.

'And now for Comcor!' said Jacob. 'It's still on, isn't it?' He hadn't stopped talking at the top of his voice.

I hesitated. Comcor was big, the biggest we had tackled yet. Maybe it was too soon. Everyone would be on their guard. And Jacob sounded so keyed up and excited; everyone was, after the success of the seal pup scenario. I should have been pleased, but somehow it worried me. Success and excitement might make us reckless — and careless.

'You've heard nothing from the managing director?' I asked Jacob. 'Nothing at all?' I lowered my voice still further. I could hear Mum moving about near the door in the other room.

'Not a thing,' said Jacob. 'And a big silence from the Minister for the Environment too. They're playing the usual waiting game.'

I took a deep breath and let it out. 'Okay,' I said at last. Why did I feel so uneasy? 'We go ahead then. I'll tell the others.'

'Have you still got the banner?' asked Jacob. Dumb question. Without the banner, there was no Comcor campaign. Toni and I had found it hanging half off the Anti-Cancer Council's offices a few weeks ago as part of the stop-smoking week. QUIT! it cried in great black letters across a white background. We kind of borrowed it for a while, pulling at the last remaining ties until they snapped, then bundling it into Toni's shopping bag, where it trailed along, more out than in. It was exactly what we needed to stop Comcor.

, 'Yes, we've got it,' I told him. 'And the ropes.'

'Great.' His voice was too quick, too loud. 'So, we meet at the bottom of the tower. At five A.M. Thursday. That's the morning. Five o'clock.'

'Sure. And Jacob — take it easy.' I tried to keep my voice casual. But every word was a warning. 'Be careful.'

'Right.'

'Who was that?' asked Mum. I tried not to jump. When I wasn't looking, she had come into the room with a pile of ironing, her hair escaping from a ponytail and getting in her eyes. Somehow, even in her crumpled jeans, she still managed to look elegant. If I scraped my hair back like that my face would look as long as a horse's, and it would make every spot and freckle stand out like neon lights. Life wasn't fair sometimes.

'Just talking to Jacob.' I went into my casual act. 'We're not watering the plants tomorrow. It's supposed to rain.' That had been in the early part of the conversation. All of us watched the weather forecast intently, hoping for wet weather. It was cold today. Who cared if all the vacationers down the road got drenched or froze to death? Lugging a couple of hundred buckets of water was murder.

'How are the plants doing?'

'Oh, good really.' I moved away from the phone. I wasn't going to ring Toni and Colin while she was there. 'Some of them are pretty big now.' And some of them were still only a couple of inches high — they could easily be crushed by a few careless feet.

A gust of wind and the first isolated pellets of rain rattled the windows in their panes. Mum moved over to the potbellied stove, which was set, ready for lighting.

'Crazy weather,' she said. 'Here we are in the middle of summer, and I'm freezing.' I nodded, and that was all she needed to bend down and put a match to the stove. In winter, it was always like this, the two of us cuddling by the fire, watching the flames play games on the walls, talking, being silent, talking again long into the night. During the hot days of summer, we took endless walks on the beach, catching up on the week apart, swapping tales about teachers and friends, trying to make each other laugh with stories both funny and sad. But winter was my favourite time. You could tell Mum anything. Well, almost anything.

'Dad won't let me stay with you,' I said. 'I mean forever.'

Mum sighed. 'Well, I didn't think he'd like the idea too much. He loves you. He wouldn't want to be apart from you.'

'He's never there,' I said. 'He wouldn't even notice I'm gone.'

Mum laughed. 'He'd notice the sudden peace!' She moved to push a log into the stove. It was burning brightly now.

'He wouldn't miss me. Just his pride would be hurt.' God, it hurt when I said it. I felt my face twist fiercely, screwed out of shape, and I wondered how much it was actually true.

'What exactly did he say?' The rain had started in earnest now, splattering all over the tin roof. I had to raise my voice to be heard.

'He just raved on about his legal rights. The usual stuff.' I stared into the fire's glow. Dad had not once said he actually wanted me to stay. 'He just told me the court order gave him custody five days a week. And that's what would happen.'

'Court orders can be changed,' said Mum. 'You're older now. You have a choice in the matter.'

I shivered a little, moving closer to the stove. It was a scary thought. I wondered what it would be like to live permanently in one place. Never having to worry about which shoes to pack or which T-shirt was in which closet. Always having the right homework in my bag. Coming home to Mum every night, teasing her about her cooking, juggling the spoons and laughing as I set the table. Being able to talk again.

'Kate says that I'm part of her family too.' I would be away at last from the silences that etched into you so that even fighting and yelling felt better.

'You are. She really does love you. You and Kate have been together a long time now.' Mum's voice always took on a kind of formal tone when she spoke about Kate. Was she jealous of Kate? I often wondered. Maybe Kate was jealous of her. Neither of them ever let on.

'What about Laura?' I asked. 'If the court order is changed, would they let Laura come with us?' But even I knew the answer. Mum took a long breath. She waited for a while.

'Tess, I'm sorry,' she said at last. 'I would be happy to. You know that. But Laura isn't related to me. The courts wouldn't allow it.'

'She's related to me!' I cried.

'And to your father and Kate. Do you think she would really leave them?'

She wouldn't, of course. 'What about weekends? Or holidays? Could she stay here then?'

Mum nodded. 'Always. As much as Kate and your dad would let her. You know that.'

But it wouldn't be enough. I always begged Kate to let Laura come and stay. Sometimes I conned Mum into ringing up Kate to do the inviting. It was always the same. Mum and Kate carefully talking, trying so hard you could hear the silences. But Dad didn't like Laura staying with Mum. And Kate, for the sake of peace, did what Dad wanted.

'It wouldn't work,' I said at last. 'It doesn't now.'

Mum sighed, not looking up, picking up some stray twigs, opening the stove, throwing them into the fire. 'I'm so sorry, Tess.' A sudden squall of rain and wind came loudly across the roof, making it difficult to hear. 'I thought it would be for the best ... with your father and Kate ... with the two of them ...' Her words seemed to ebb and flow with the wind. I couldn't see her face. 'I had hoped so much I was doing the right thing ... giving you up ...'

There was silence for a long time. I didn't move. I had always wondered why Dad had got custody of me for most of the week. I couldn't imagine him asking for it. He certainly wouldn't have taken time off from his Happy Retirement talks or revising Act 79, 247 of Parliament to stand up in court and fight for custody. So Mum must have offered the compromise. Had she really thought that two parents were better than one — especially when one of them was always away?

The wind gusted and rattled at the windows. I leaned forward, straining to hear. 'It was different then. Michael was at home more ...' She seemed to know what I was thinking. 'And Kate's so very clever ... so kind ... I thought it would be better ...' Mum was murmuring into the shadows. I wasn't sure she was talking to me anymore. Rain was pouring down on the roof, pelting loudly. 'I don't know now ...' I wasn't sure I had even heard her right.

Chapter 12

There were 227 steps up the narrow metal ladder alongside Comcor's chimney. Just 227 steps in a howling wind and predawn darkness until we reached the inspection balcony, which circled near the tower's top. The backpack with the banner stuffed inside bumped against me every step, the wind trying hard to tug it free. I didn't complain. I could have been carrying Colin's backpack. It had bricks in it.

The rungs of the ladder were covered with black carbon dust and God knows what other toxic stuff from the chimney. The higher we went, the more slippery each rung got.

'Careful now,' panted Colin. 'I'm just getting to the balcony.' With a heave, his legs disappeared sideways from sight, and we heard a clang as he dropped his backpack to the floor. Fighting the wind and a stupid, suicidal urge to look down, the rest of us followed.

'Hell,' panted Jacob. 'It's a long way up here.' Spread out far below was the town, the streetlights on the roads ribboning their way among houses and shops. Beyond stretched the sea, where the wind had whipped dark water into whitecaps just visible in the distance.

'What a view!' Toni was trying to hold her hair out of her eyes with both hands, but the wind was winning. She leaned over and looked at the ground below. 'It's sure a long way down.'

'Is the rope still there?' asked Colin. We'd needed the rope to climb the first twenty feet — Comcor's ladder hadn't started until about then. I'd checked it all out last week. It had taken days to figure everything out.

'I guess so,' said Toni. She didn't look again. Surreptitiously she edged backwards until her body rested against the main trunk of the smokestack. Black soot instantly smeared her jumper. She didn't seem to care.

'Come on,' I said. 'We'd better get to work.' I hadn't recovered from the climb up, but looking down was scrambling all sorts of things in my stomach and brain. I opened my backpack, grabbed one end of the banner, and started pulling. 'Take the other end, will you,' I said to Colin. But the wind beat him to it, tugging at it playfully, spinning it high into the air out of our reach. I held fast to the ties while the rest of it furled and flapped and everyone stumbled around the balcony trying to play catch with it.

'We don't have to tie it down,' called Toni. 'We'll just leave you up here with it.'

'Hurry up, will you!' The ties were starting to cut into my hands.

'Nearly got you now!' Colin was reaching up for an end, victory in sight.

A sudden rush of wind swirled around the tower. Colin lunged high, but the banner twisted itself from his grasp, and suddenly I felt material cut into my hands like knives.

'Look out!' yelled Toni. But like a huge alien enemy, the banner hurled itself upwards. It hovered above, twisting to gain momentum, and then suddenly it cut down, hurling through the air, aiming directly at Colin. There was a rushing sound, a sudden crack like a whip as the end lashed across his face.

'Arrrrhh!' he screamed, and reeled backwards. And then there were other voices screaming, mine too. For where Colin stood, there was no railing, no metal, no bars to stop his body. Only the empty space above the ladder and the endless, terrible fall to the ground.

'ARRRRHH!' The cry was all around us. 'ARRRRHH!' And only Colin could move, hands clawing at his face, trying to dig out the pain while his legs moved backwards, still backwards towards the terrible edge ...

There were two frames of living going on in my mind. Two different forms of reality. I can still see the first one always. The one where Colin takes one tiny step more. Backwards. And suddenly his body is tilting across the edge, stretching farther and farther back until his feet are wrenched from the platform and his body spreads out into the air, falling, gathering speed, hurtling towards the ground far far away. We wait forever for the thump as his body smashes into the earth below.

Then there is the other frame, where I see Jacob moving forward, crying out. Too slow to reach Colin. Too slow by an eternity. But it doesn't matter now. For Colin was sinking forwards — towards us — forwards onto the platform. Sinking onto his knees, his hands still clutching his face, falling still forwards, safe for a tiny moment. Safer still when Jacob reached him at last, dragging him forwards still more, holding him fast.

Which version was reality?

'Oh my God! My God!' cried Colin. Blood was spreading through his fingers.

Suddenly we were all moving and shouting. I flung myself against Colin and Jacob, crying words into the wind that were lost forever. They were meaningless anyway. All that was real was to hold fast to Colin, arms aching as they wrapped around him to guard against the wind and the pain and the sickening vision of the fall that might have been forever.

Another eternity passed. Light, cold and gray from the false dawn, crept over us. Someone was stirring uncertainly against my body.

'I'm okay,' Colin said. 'I'm okay.' His voice and his body were shaking uncontrollably.

'I thought ... ' Toni began. 'When you were ...' She didn't finish. One hand clutched Jacob's. The other was wound tightly into Colin's overalls.

'You're safe,' I said. 'Safe.' It was all I could say. I had never known before how closely tragedy lurked behind life. Never understood how one tiny step backwards or forwards could mean the difference between life or death.

It took us nearly twenty minutes to hang

the banner. It should have taken only five of course. We had all wanted to get out of there as fast as possible. But Colin had insisted we finish the job.

'It's what we came to do,' he said stubbornly. In the gray light you could see clearly the welt cutting deeply right across his face. It was still oozing blood. But he wouldn't leave.

In the end we made him sit huddled against the tower while the rest of us fumbled and shuffled the banner into place, hanging on tightly in about three places to anyone who went anywhere near the edge. Toni lay on the material while the rest of us tied on the bricks to weigh it down. Everything took so long, and our fingers felt as thick and clumsy as our brains. The banner lay quietly as we worked, as if contrite. Edging carefully forwards, we tied the top strips of material to the edge of the railing. Finally, we eased the bricks with the rest of the banner attached over the edge, where it flapped gently against the rails.

'Will you look at that,' said Jacob. All of us were panting and covered with sweat and black slime. But he was shielding his eyes, looking far to the east. At the horizon, the first tiny rays of the rising sun had coloured the sky. Even as we watched, more rays followed, and more, streaking the horizon red and gold. The first rounded edge of the sun followed, glowing, touching the world with light.

'It's beautiful,' whispered Toni. The wind carried her words away into the distance. "Like a rainbow of red and magic.'

'"Red sky at morning, sailor take warning",' Colin said.

'Cautious Colin to the last.' Jacob laughed and punched him lightly on the arm.

The world spread below seemed covered in soft crimson. Soon the streetlights would flicker and die out, their night's work done. The world would start to move again, people would be stretching in their beds, gulping down breakfast toast, getting into their cars. Soon, too, the roads would hold ribbons of cars, all heading into the city, all passing directly below the tower where we stood. We wouldn't be there of course. But our hopes would. Stretched out over the railing, as Comcor's chimney belched forth its smoke once again, our banner would remain. QUIT! it would demand. And people would look up and laugh and maybe remember.

Colin was looking down at it now, a grin spreading slowly across his face.

'It looks great!' he said. He reached across to Jacob and gave him a high five.

'Fantastic!' he shouted above the wind.

'You mean fan-bloody-tastic!' Jacob laughed and shouted in return.

'We did it,' I said. I was talking only to myself, but Toni grabbed me in a hug.

'We sure did! We're brilliant!' she cried, and she pulled Colin and Jacob into the hug, holding us all together.

'We can make a difference,' I whispered. A lone car was driving up the street towards the tower. The QUIT! banner flapped gaily. 'We can!' I shouted for us all. Another car followed it and then another. They pulled up under the chimney, and people got out. I was grinning, stupidly, insanely smiling, as I watched them. They were looking up at us and pointing. I half lifted a hand to wave.

Then suddenly I was crying out, wrenching myself free of Toni, pushing her urgently towards the ladder.

'Come on!' I shouted. She wasn't moving! 'Run!' I yelled. More people were gathering around the cars. I pushed at Colin, forcing him towards the steps. 'We've got to get out of here! Run!'

'What is it?' Colin didn't move. He didn't understand! Frantically, I pointed to the cars and the faces beneath us. 'We'll be trapped up here!' I yelled.

'No! It can't be!' Now Toni had seen them and was racing for the ladder. 'No!' she cried again.

And then a loudhailer was pulled from one of the cars and a voice rang out. Even against the wind, we could hear it clearly.

'You four people up there! This is the police. Come down slowly now. It's over. Come down slowly and there won't be any trouble.'

It was 227 steps down, down, down to failure.

Chapter 13

Step down, step down. There was a sick cold numbness around my heart that said this couldn't be happening. Not after we had been so close to disaster. So close to victory. Step down, step down. I could hear Toni's breath coming in ragged gulps below me. Beneath her, I could hear Jacob's and Colin's feet, scuffling against the metal rungs. Step down, down, down. Everything moved strangely, as if our hands and feet were a long, long way from the brain.

'Careful now,' came the amplified voice from the cars. 'Take it slowly.' There was a pause from Toni below. I waited, concentrating on trying to breathe. Movement again, different this time, and I found my feet feeling for steps that weren't there. A rope brushed against me. The last part of the journey. My legs wrapped around it, my hands warm, burning as I let myself slide down. Then other hands were around my body and someone was carefully holding me as I stumbled onto the ground at last.

'We were just trying to help,' I tried to explain to the face above the hands. Everything seemed blurred around the edges. 'Just trying to stop Comcor. It's poison ...'

The face nodded. 'You can tell us all about it later,' it said. 'At the police station.' I felt myself moving forwards. There were other voices around me.

'Call ahead, get a medico ...'

'Just kids ...'

'... contact the parents ...'

'You can't!' That was Toni crying. 'No! Don't tell my mother! Please!' I struggled to see her. There were other faces around me now.

'It's my fault,' I told them. 'Let her go. It's all my fault.'

'We'll sort it out at the station,' one said.

'Please!' I begged. 'It was all my idea. They wouldn't have done it except for me.'

'Into the car now,' a voice said. A hand pushed gently behind my head and back.

'It's my fault!' I cried. 'Let them go!'

Colin was sitting in the car, a woman police officer beside him. The welt on his face was dark red now, spreading. A tiny patch of my brain cleared.

'Colin's hurt!' I cried. 'You must help him!'

'At the station,' the police officer said. 'We've radioed ahead for a doctor.' Hands were still pushing me, urging me into the car. I obeyed. I couldn't think, didn't know what else to do.

'It was the chimney, you see,' I told the police officer. 'We had to do something.'

'It'll be all right, dear,' she said. I tried to focus on her face. She didn't look angry or cross, but I don't know if her face could smile either. 'We'll sort it out soon.' It was all routine to her.

Colin was leaning against the back seat of the car, as if all the bones had dissolved inside him. His face looked ghastly. I leaned across the police officer to speak to him. And then didn't know what to say.

'I'm sorry,' I managed to get out at last. I scooped the air with my hands, trying to gather words. Colin had always been the worrier, always the one wondering what would happen if things went wrong or we got caught. I had been forging full speed ahead, dreaming of changing the world and covering ourselves with glory. Now his worst fears had come true. Because of me. 'Sorry,' I said again.

Colin shook his head without raising it from the seat. 'We were all in it,' he said. Somehow that made the guilt worse.

'How's your face?' I asked. I only had to look to see that he must be in pain.

'It's okay,' he said. He raised his hand to the bloody welt biting across his face and closed his eyes. It was like him not to complain.

'What will your parents say?' I asked. Wasn't that what we were all thinking? On the other side of the compound, I could just make out Toni and Jacob, sitting in another police car, a huge beefy sergeant wedged between them. They would be asking each other the same question.

Colin didn't open his eyes. His shoulders just managed to move in what might have been a shrug. 'Who knows?' he said. And then a small smile began at his lips. His face twitched a little on the good side, and at last he opened his eyes and looked at me. 'At least they'll know now why I'm so lousy on the guitar,' he said.

The first car was pulling away. Toni and

Jacob were in the back, white-faced and still. The streetlights flickered and died out. Cars were starting to come onto the roads, heading for work and the city. As our car began to move, I craned my neck to look up. Far above, the QUIT! banner flapped gaily in the wind. On the ladder, against the smokestack, two men in police uniform were climbing towards it.

Chapter 14

It was cold at the police station. They had taken Colin to see the doctor. I could hear Toni's voice in a room off to the side.

'We didn't do any harm ... we didn't ...'

There was a desk and another face and uniform.

'Empty your pockets, please.'

A pen, some paper ...

'Name? Address?'

A few bits of cotton. A Band-Aid, scuffed and bent.

'Parents' names? Address? Phone number?'

Two sticks of chewing gum. I never used it.

They were filling out forms, pressing hard to make the triplicate come through.

Now I was waiting in a room that smelt of old smoke, new, cheap carpet, and fear. Or had I taken that last smell into the room?

'It won't be long now, dear.' The police officer from the car had been waiting with me,
saying those words for what seemed like hours.
She had brought me a coffee and snagged the
only magazine in the room. There were no pictures on the wall, only a tape recorder, a table,
hard chairs, nothing to do or say. 'Your parents
will be here any minute now.' The woman actually smiled at me. Did she think she was offering comfort?

'Which parents did they tell?' I asked. She
looked surprised.

'How many do you have?'

'Two mothers. One father.' I didn't go into
details.

'We probably notified all of them,' she said.
'We usually do.' Maybe they hadn't. Maybe just
Mum would turn up. Or Kate. Maybe Dad
would have left early for the Canberra conference. Maybe.

'What's the charge against her?' I heard his
voice far down the corridor, loud and harsh.

'Trespassing,' came a rumble of a voice. 'Bill
posting. Possibly theft of a banner.'

'Is she all right?' That was Kate of course.
And then Dad came through the doorway.
Even at this hour, his uniform of suit and silk
tie was immaculate, his face carefully set into

the public mould he used whenever a reporter asked him a question he thought in bad taste. He stopped just inside the room.

'What's this all about, Tess?' he asked. Kate came into the room, brushing past him, making straight to me. She was holding out her arms. And then footsteps came running down the corridor, Mum burst into the room, and suddenly they were both holding me, talking to me, drawing me in to comfort and protection. Tears burst out of me. I hadn't even felt them coming.

'Oh, my darling,' said Mum. Her arms tightened around me.

'Tess, my dear Tess.' Kate was stroking my hair.

'My love, you're safe. We have you.'

'Are you all right? You poor darling.'

'Tess. Oh, Tess ...'

The front of Mum's shirt was plastered with tears. My nose was blocked, and I could hardly breathe. I struggled out of Mum's and Kate's arms at last and smiled waterlogged up at them. Kate found me a hankie. I blew and dabbed and blew again. And then suddenly I laughed and hugged them both fiercely, insanely, feeling impossibly happy.

'We'd like to talk to you now.' There was a click as the police sergeant switched on the tape recorder. Reality came back with a shocking jolt. 'What exactly were you doing up there?' he asked. He didn't sound angry, just kind of neutral, but I looked at Dad and went cold all over.

'I'm here.' Mum slid her arm around me and leaned across to whisper the words into my hair like she always did. 'I'll always be here.' On the other side, Kate was holding my hand tightly, her head turned so I could see her face. She nodded and smiled.

'It's okay,' she said. 'We'll help you.' The tape recorder whirled and waited.

'It was the chimney ... ' I tried to explain. 'Comcor is putting all this poison into our air. Every day. And no one seems to care.' I stopped. Mum's arm moved, stroking up and down my back, as if she were soothing a frightened cat.

'Go on,' said the sergeant.

The woman police officer was sitting upright now, taking notes.

I swallowed and tried to find the right words. 'It was supposed to make people laugh, you see.' Was I making sense? 'And start them asking questions about Comcor too.' The woman looked up and nodded at me. She looked like she was about to smile again. Dad was looking at his watch.

'Where did you get the banner?' That was the sergeant again.

'From the Anti-Cancer Council. It was hanging half off the wall outside their office.'

'So you took it down?'

'It would have come off anyway!' I said.

'And whose idea was all this?' The sergeant had still not raised his voice. I looked up at him. He had been talking to Colin and Jacob and Toni too. You could see that. He knew.

'Mine,' I said. 'I was the leader. It was my idea.'

'You!' Dad suddenly took a step forward and threw out his hands. I felt Mum and Kate move closer. 'I might have known!' he said bitterly.

'Please, sir,' said the sergeant. 'It doesn't help if we lose our temper.' He didn't look like he ever lost his. Dad checked his watch again.

'It was meant to help,' I said. 'A kind of a joke.'

'Great!' Dad swung his arms wide again. 'I'm about to miss the conference of the heads of state because my daughter thinks putting banners on chimneys is a joke!'

'Michael ...' said Kate. But I pulled myself free of her and Mum.

'You don't have to miss the conference!' I

told him. 'Get on the plane and go to it! I don't need you here!'

'Huh!' Dad suddenly flared to shouting mode. 'You're under arrest and you say you don't need me! Think again, my girl.'

'Ah, technically, sir, she's not under arrest.' The sergeant's voice sounded really soft. 'Comcor and the Anti-Cancer Council will not be pressing charges. We've talked to them both already.'

'Then what's she doing here?' Dad struggled to control his voice, arms folded, politician's displeasure in place.

'Let's just call it a warning,' said the sergeant. 'Now that we know the full story.'

'You mean she can go home?' asked Mum. 'Now?'

'Really?' I could only manage a croak. Was it possible I would be allowed to walk out of here? Just like that?

'The rest of the group have already left. Your friend will have a sore face for a while though,' he said to me.

'Is he ... ?' I couldn't get any more words out.

'He's fine.' The sergeant was standing up, shuffling papers. 'We'll just get you to sign the release papers and the official caution, sir. And the mother too.' He looked across at Mum and Kate, unable to choose between them. 'And then you can be on your way.' He was trying to herd Dad from the room. But Dad wouldn't budge. He looked at me and shook his head.

'Why, Tess?' he asked. 'Why did you do it?'

What could I say? He would never understand. I shrugged.

'I just wanted to do something to change things,' I said. The tears had come back. I wiped them away. 'I don't know. Maybe help make the world a better place to live in.'

Dad stopped. He looked puzzled, head tilted as if trying to remember. 'A better place ...' For once his voice was quiet.

'You'd better hurry,' said Kate. 'Your plane ...'

But Dad seemed strangely reluctant to move. He just stood there, staring at me. 'I used to say that,' he said. And then he turned and went out the door.

Chapter 15

'Another hot chocolate?' It had once been a favourite daydream. Kate and Mum and me sitting in some cosy little café, sharing coffee and confidences. This café had old linoleum on the floor, chipped tables, and a loud cappuccino machine that made it more clattering than cosy. But it was a start.

For minutes at a time, great surges of happiness flooded over me, making me grin and laugh crazily. Colin was alive, we hadn't been arrested or charged or thrown in jail. We had been given a chance ...

And then I remembered that our names were recorded at the police station. That nothing would ever be the same again. Right now, Colin and Toni and Jacob would be facing their parents and trying to explain. There would be shouting and biting words in all their homes — because of me. I wondered if Jacob's parents would be angry. Jacob had always wanted to know. He would find out for sure now.

'Tess?' It was Kate. 'I asked did you want another hot chocolate?'

'Mmmm? Oh yes!' Another surge of happiness hit me. I smiled hugely at Kate and Mum. 'Yes please!' Dad was gone, and my own shouting match wouldn't start for days, until he got back from Canberra. I wanted this moment to just go on and on and on.

'You're lucky you've got two mums,' the woman police officer had said as Mum and Kate both signed the form to get my release. They had to squash their names to fit into the space beside Dad's.

'I guess so.' I had never really thought about it like that. Sitting in the café I found myself grinning like one of those slobbery dogs — all sloppy jaws and clumsy tail and forever friendly.

'Where's Laura?' I asked suddenly.

'I got a neighbour to come over,' said Kate. 'She was still asleep when we left.'

'She'll be worried.' I sighed. 'Maybe we'd better go.' I hated the idea. But I also hated for Laura to worry.

'She's fine,' said Kate. 'I rang her from the

police station.' I hadn't noticed. Everything had seemed hazy and unreal from the time I had started climbing up the rope under Comcor's smokestack. Only the image of Colin, crying out, clutching his face and stumbling on the edge of the platform was clear. I shivered.

'Why the name?' Mum put her hand over mine. 'The Green Guerrillas?' She was biting into another doughnut. Normally, she never ate them.

'It was Toni's idea,' I said. 'When I said we would run guerrilla campaigns, she came up with the name.'

'You mean there were other things before this?' asked Kate. I looked at her carefully and then at Mum. Would they be mad? I watched their faces; they just seemed curious.

'We wrote letters to politicians. And put up posters in pharmacies to protest against using animals for testing makeup.'

'Oh, yes.' Mum knew all too well my stance on that.

'And in the supermarkets too.' I checked their faces again. 'You know: "Go Green Clean" and "Are You Eating Tuna — or Dolphin???"'

'Oh heavens!' Mum started to laugh. 'That was you? I wondered why you always wanted to go shopping with me lately.'

'Me too!' Kate was laughing as well. Obviously both had been rather puzzled by my sudden urge to help with the groceries.

'But that's been going on for months,' said Mum. I nodded.

'Toni and Colin and Jacob did it too?' Kate's head was tilted as always, hair escaping her bun, a tiny smile around her lips. I nodded again. I just hoped the others had had the sense not to mention any of our other activities to the police. I certainly hadn't brought it up.

'The supermarkets have been driven mad by that!'

'No wonder you called yourselves guerrillas,' said Kate.

'The Green Guerrillas.' Mum said the name thoughtfully. Suddenly she got up and walked over to the pile of magazines supplied by the café. She picked out the local paper, and my heart skipped a few beats and moved into rapid mode. I knew what was coming next.

'That too,' I said as she spread the front page over the table before us.

'Is that *your* group?' Kate was almost incredulous as she pointed to the picture of the sealer, leering in menace as his club swung directly over the head of the helpless seal. The photographer had known his stuff — he'd caught it at just the right moment.

I pointed to the photograph. 'Colin,' I said, touching the sealer. 'And me.' In the photo I looked more like a seal pup than I knew.

'Oh my God.' Mum shook her head. I don't think she knew whether to laugh or panic. 'Where did you learn all this? The planning, the ideas? How did you get all the newspapers to cover it?'

I looked at her. 'Where do you think?' I asked. There was only one media expert in the family. All I had to do was watch and listen and learn. Mum frowned, eyes looking through the cappuccino machine and beyond, and then she nodded slowly.

'Michael,' she said. 'I see.'

'Oh Lord!' Kate leaned back in her chair and ran her fingers through her hair. 'What's he going to say about all this!'

'You can't tell him!' I half rose out of my chair. 'He'd kill me!' I cried.

Kate wasn't looking at me. Her eyes had sought out Mum's and locked there. It seemed forever before someone spoke.

'I hardly ever see Michael,' said Mum. 'I won't be mentioning it.'

Kate gave a tiny nod. 'I think we'll be busy

talking about other things,' she said. 'It's not worth bringing this up.'

I slumped back in my chair, relieved. Life could get worse in a hurry if Dad knew about things like seal pups and supermarkets. I yawned hugely. I was exhausted.

'Come on,' said Kate.

'Time to go home,' said Mum.

Home, to sleep and rest and somehow try to make some order out of the world. I yawned again and began to stand up. Mum was holding out her hand, and Kate was moving to take my other arm. Suddenly I stopped moving. Home, wonderful home, yes. But which home?

Mum realised first. Her hand dropped.

'I'm sorry,' she said to Kate. 'I forgot she's with you ...'

'Perhaps she needs to be with you.' Kate looked at me. Her voice was gentle. 'After all, she's your daughter.'

No one was moving now. The waitress came over, slipped the bill onto the table, and left with a curious stare.

At last Mum gave a sigh and turned to me. 'I guess this is where it starts,' she said. What was she talking about? 'If you're old enough to take on half the supermarkets in town and

Comcor to boot, you're old enough to make your own decisions.'

'Stop it!' I cried. 'I don't want to choose between you!' I realised with a jolt that the police officer was right — I really did have two mothers. I *was* lucky. But if I chose to go with Mum, Kate would feel so terribly hurt. And if I went with Kate ...

I felt panic, cold and hot, wrap around me.

'Mum ...' I moved to her side and held tight against her. 'What am I going to do?'

'Oh, Tess,' she murmured. Her hands tried to give me strength as she stroked my hair. 'I wish I could tell you. I wish I knew.'

I clung tighter. There was something else too. 'All my things are at Kate's,' I whispered.

'Darling, that's not important. You can live without a few white T-shirts for once.'

I was shaking my head, stepping back so she could see more clearly. *'All of my things!'* I muttered fiercely.

'The dreamcatcher.' Kate's voice came, strangely muted. I looked across at her. Her face was lifted, chin set and lips held determinedly into a smile. Hair wisped in her eyes, and she brushed it back again. For so long now I had watched that gesture, over breakfast as we discussed books and homework, at night as she whirled around the kitchen cooking dinner while I shelled peas and filled her in on the latest soap operas and love affairs and gossip from school. 'I can bring it over,' she said. 'Don't worry. I'll bring it.'

'No.' I stood up, letting go of Mum's hands. For over ten years Kate had made sure I was always a part of her family. Even when Laura was born, I'd never felt left out — she'd taught me how to dress the baby and hold her and even give her a bottle. We had walked to the park and taken it in turns to push Laura on the swings. We'd gone shopping together, shared movies, and walked to school on Laura's first day, each holding a hand on either side. Kate had worked so hard to make us a family. And I owed her something in return. 'I'm coming with you,' I said. I looked at Mum. 'But would you pick me up in the morning?'

'Of course.' She reached out and gripped my shoulder fiercely. She understood what I was doing. Somehow I had known she would.

'Are you sure?' Kate asked. 'I mean ...'

I walked over to her, chairs and tables getting in the way.

'We're sure,' I said. 'I love you too!' She put her arms around me and held tight. It was only when I felt tears drop onto my shoulder that I realised she was crying.

'Thank you,' she whispered. Had I never told her before? In all those years? Surely I had? I felt her look across to Mum. 'Thank you,' she whispered again.

None of us had even mentioned the weather. Not once.

Chapter 16

Mum came to pick me up early from Kate's on Friday morning — a real change in routine. Kate offered her a coffee — stranger and stranger. That was the last Laura and I saw of them for two hours.

'What do you think they're talking about?' asked Laura. We were in the kitchen, eyeing Kate and Mum through the doorway. Only a few stray words filtered through.

'... police caution ... schooling ...'

'... counselling ... Michael ...'

'... rebellion ...'

'What do you think?' I said.

'How did you have the nerve?' asked Laura. She had been really shocked when Kate and I came home and told her the rest of the story. She had wanted to know if the police had searched me, taken my fingerprints, and put me in a jail cell.

'Maybe the Comcor smokestack wasn't such a good idea,' I said. 'But the rest of it ...' I shrugged, frowning. 'It's important,' I tried to explain. 'We weren't doing it just for fun.'

'What will you do now?'

'I don't know,' I said. 'It depends on Dad.' I fought down a wave of depression. 'And on them.' I nodded at the door where Kate and Mum were still going strong. Maybe it was a good thing the politeness barrier had come down at last. But I didn't particularly enjoy being the major topic of conversation.

I practically had to drag Mum out to the car in the end. She was all hyped up and excited. Too much coffee, I suppose.

'Well?' I demanded. 'What have you decided?'

'Decided?' Mum looked at me strangely.

'About me!' I said.

Mum smiled and took her hand off the steering wheel to touch my shoulder. I kept my eyes straight ahead. Someone had to make sure we didn't run off the road. 'You make your own decisions,' Mum said. 'You've proved that surely. We can only make suggestions and back you up.'

'I'm not giving up the Green Guerrillas!' I announced. I looked over at her. She didn't say anything. Suddenly, turning a left corner seemed to take all her concentration. 'Though I might just give up being arrested,' I said. It didn't take much to make Mum laugh today. She cracked up.

'Glad to hear that.' Her fingers drummed against the steering wheel. She seemed reckless, happy, sad — everything all at once. 'Oh, Tess,' she said. 'You have so many strengths. So many skills. Don't waste them all. Please!'

'I'm not wasting them,' I said. 'The group is really important to me.'

'But you're letting everything else go sour!' Mum's voice was full of yearning. 'Home, your swimming, all your schoolwork — '

'I knew it would get back to school,' I said.

'Think about afterwards,' she urged. 'What do you really want to do with your life after you finish your schooling?'

I didn't have to think about it. 'I'll work on cleaning up the ocean. Maybe join Greenpeace or something like that. As a marine ecologist.' Too late I saw where she was heading me. Marine ecologists needed top university degrees. And university degrees needed ...

'School,' I confirmed gloomily. I'd fallen right into that one.

Mum laughed. 'Well, it's not a bad first step,' she said.

'It didn't take you two hours to figure all that out,' I said. 'What else were you talking about with Kate?'

'Er ...' Mum suddenly looked confused. 'I don't really know. About each other, I guess.' A little smile played around her lips, and then she grew serious again. 'There is something else we talked about,' she said.

I felt myself go rigid. 'What?'

'We thought maybe it was time ...' She trailed off, thinking. 'The custody arrangements,' she said. 'You might want to change them.' I kept my eyes on the road and didn't say anything. 'You're old enough now,' Mum added. 'You have a choice in the matter.'

I felt something lurch and swirl inside me. It was the same old question. Sometimes I needed so much to live with Mum. To feel safe, secure. The feeling welled up more and more often now. Yet how could I leave Laura? And Kate? How could I live with Mum and be happy without them?

'More decisions.' I sighed. And maybe more possibilities that someone would get hurt.

'It doesn't have to be one or the other,' said Mum. 'Maybe just a different arrangement. Come here for more of the holidays, like we said. Or spend a month or two here, and then go back.'

I felt my face twisting. 'What can I do?' I wailed. 'I keep thinking and thinking. Nothing works!'

Mum was pulling into the driveway at home. She switched off the engine and moved over on the seat to hold me tight. I felt her breath against my face. Funny how she could just touch you, and somehow you felt she was sharing her strength with you.

'Why don't we just try out a few different ways?' she said. 'See what works. A few months one style. A few months another way. Then it's not forever.'

'But by the time we try them all out,' I sniffed, 'it'll be time I left home. Both homes,' I corrected.

'So?' Mum grinned. 'End of problem,' she said. Somehow, even when I was crying, she could always make me laugh.

Chapter 17

We should have bought bulk rates for the telephone on Friday. It was never on the hook for more than a few minutes all day.

Toni was the first to check in.

'What are you doing over there?' she demanded. 'It's Friday.'

'Er ... things are changing,' I said. I didn't want to explain further. 'How did you know I was here?'

'Laura. I rang there of course. Do you know I've been grounded for a whole month?'

'Was your mum really mad?' According to Toni, she could be incredibly strict sometimes.

'Furified.' Things were bad when Toni started to create new words. It wasn't too hard to guess what she meant. 'It's kind of funny though.' She sounded puzzled. 'All of our friends and family have been calling in. And she's been talking nonstop. But ... well, you know how I don't understand her languages that much.'

'I know.' Toni's mother had been born in Europe and spoke at least four languages with ease. She worked as an interpreter for some high-class company. When she got excited, she often switched from Italian to German to Greek without noticing. But Toni had been born on the other side of the world and didn't understand much except English and a lot of hand movements.

'It's weird. But I could swear she sounds almost proud. And everyone is shaking their heads and patting me on the back at the same time. I mean she grounds me for a month and then she goes and tells everyone about it. I don't get it.'

'Sounds like you got off lightly to me.' I thought of Dad, sitting together with all the heads of state, discussing funding allocations, state grants, and big budgets. He would be right in his element — until he had to fly home tomorrow for Laura's competition, and then blow the lid off my world. I swallowed hard, clamping down quickly on the lump in my throat.

'You call a month of being under house arrest light?' demanded Toni. Her voice rose.

'No friends, no beach, no trips into town. Hell, she's even unplugged the TV!'

~

'I told my folks everything,' said Colin. 'It was strange. They didn't seem that surprised.'

'Do you think maybe they'd known already?' Was it possible Colin had been right about being so cautious? Maybe his parents could read minds or something.

'I'm not sure.' I could almost hear him shrug.'But you know the picture of you and me doing the seal cub act? Mum had cut it out from the paper. It's been pinned to our fridge ever since last week.'

'Maybe they could offer you acting lessons,' I said. 'Instead of learning the guitar.'

'Fat chance!' Colin snorted. 'But you know what? Dad said he had always wondered about the Comcor tower.'

'Good!' I said. 'If we get a few more people asking questions — '

'Huh!' said Colin. 'The only questions he's been asking at the moment are the ones about me. He also reckons that if I'm old enough to climb towers, I'm old enough to mow the lawn from now on. Plus help more with the cooking. And Mom's been going on and on about my face, and panicking in case I'm scarred for life or something. They were just getting warmed up when you rang. Great timing, Tess.'

'Glad to be of service,' I said.

'Yeah. Well I think I'll lie low for the rest of the day. No, make that the rest of the week. Just in case.'

~

'Mum and Dad made me go through the release papers we signed at the police station word by word.' Jacob still sounded shaken. 'Do you know that it goes in a file? And it stays there forever!'

I felt my stomach churn up into my throat. I hadn't known that.

'It shouldn't matter, should it? I mean, we're not exactly hardened criminals. Unless you're planning to rob a few banks soon.' I tried to keep it light, but my own throat was pretty dry.

'I guess not. But still ...'

'How much do your parents know?' I changed the subject.

'Well, uhm ...' He hesitated. 'I didn't tell them about the mayor and the seal pup demonstration. But I mentioned in passing we were trying to get supermarkets not to stock some products.'

'Did you tell them how?'

'Er ... no.' And Jacob had been the one who thought our parents would understand. Funny how it worked out. 'But I did tell them about all the letters we wrote,' he said. 'Mum and Dad were quite interested in that. They've even offered to help.'

'Hey, that would be terrific!' Maybe all the politicians and company managers and PR people would be more willing to listen to adults.

'Yeah. We can write the letters on Dad's computer at work. Send off lots more that way. And guess what. It's got a spelling check on it!'

Maybe it wasn't the end of the Green Guerrillas after all. Maybe we were just at the beginning.

~

Laura was the last person I talked to, late in the afternoon, when Kate would have been moving like quicksilver in the kitchen preparing dinner and Laura should have been curled up on her bed reading as always.

'I just rang to wish you good luck for tomorrow,' I told her. 'But we'll be seeing you anyway.'

'Thanks,' she said. 'Dad rang too.' I could hear it in her voice; she was all keyed up and thrilled. 'He said he had a meeting with the

NSW premier in the morning, but he'd cut it short and be there in time to see me.' Heady stuff for Dad, toast and talks with premiers for breakfast. He'd better not have a second cup of coffee though. Planes didn't wait.

'He'd better be,' I said. 'Or the next time he wants to see you compete, he'll have to fly all the way to Brisbane.' That's where the Australian Championships were being held.

'Oh, Tess ...' She was trying to laugh. Trying really hard.

'I'll tell you what I'll do,' I said. 'I'll bring our old stuffed teddy to the gym. The big one. Dress it in a suit with a tie around its neck, and it can take Dad's seat until he gets there. You'll hardly notice the difference.'

Another laugh. But somehow I wished she hadn't. It came out wrong somehow, all tight and brittle.

'And I'll rig up a tape recorder. It'll say "I know you can do it" every two minutes.' I was practically gibbering now. 'And when you win, I'll just switch it to past tense. "I knew you could do it. I knew you could do it".' No laugh. Only her voice, far away, faint down the telephone line.

'He might not come,' she whispered. 'He might not ever come ...'

'What do you mean?' I asked. She wasn't making sense.

'Sometimes I think he'll get on a plane ... and just keep going.' Her voice was tiny, almost impossible to hear. 'He might never come back.'

'What?' Was I hearing her right? 'Why would he do that?'

'He might just want to ... stay away,' she whispered. 'Forever. That's what I always dream, you know.'

'Oh, Laura!' I was holding the phone tightly, pressing it against my face, as if she could feel me, touch me. 'Why?' I cried. 'Why didn't you tell me?' Something inside me was swelling, throbbing, threatening to burst.

'Everyone has nightmares,' she said. 'Don't they?'

Chapter 18

The blue teddy bear sat with an old school blazer for a suit and a strip of red material around its neck for a tie.

'Dad will be here soon,' said Laura loudly. It was the first time she had said his name. We'd been at the gym for an hour now, signing Laura in, talking to her coach, pushing through the crowd to find seats, watching and waiting as the seniors went through their routines, spinning high above the trampolines. 'He'll be coming any minute now,' she said again. Her voice started out firmly but then just seemed to trail off to a whisper at the end.

'Of course he will,' said Kate. She shifted closer on the bench and put an arm around Laura's shoulders. Laura sat rigid and unbending. It looked strange, the two of them sitting like that in the crowd, as if they were strangers forced to touch.

'The planes are always late.' Laura's feet were dangling short above the floor, toes pointed, stiff.

'I've never known one to be on time yet,' said Mum. She leaned over to smile at Laura, but Laura was watching the door.

'Oh! Ah!' from the crowd as one of the senior team members came out of a double 'sault too close to the edge. His knees bent, killing the bounce, and he raised a disappointed hand to the judges, bailing out. I looked at Laura. 'What do you think about when you're on the tramp?' I asked. 'Does it feel like flying?'

'Flying?' She looked at me blankly. 'I just try and concentrate on my form. Getting height, pointing my toes.' She paused for a long time. 'Sometimes though ...' She drifted into silence. Everyone was trying to think of something to say.

'The double back 'sault will be fine,' Laura murmured. Was she talking to us?

'It looks great,' I told her.

'Just fine ...' Laura wasn't hearing me at all. She just kept nodding to herself.

Near the middle of the gym, the rest of Laura's squad had set up camp, spreading sleeping bags on the floor, talking and laughing as they did one another's hair and compared routines. They looked happy, excited. There was a stirring among them as a competitor started out for the trampolines, slapping hands against friends as he went. They had finished with the senior competitors now and were starting on the juniors. Dad was cutting it close. Real close.

'Come on,' I said to Laura. 'Let's go down and join your team.' It was terrible waiting up there.

The group was a sea of blue and white uniforms and high-pitched chatter. The coach nodded at her and people called hello. Laura didn't say a word.

'Want me to do your hair?' a girl asked. Laura shrank back and shook her head.

'I'll do it,' I said quickly. 'Lend me a brush, will you?'

There was movement and a reshuffling as more of the squad moved out.

'We're on next!' a teammate called. Laura nodded. Her eyes shifted to where Mum and Kate sat, now with two empty seats beside them, and then to the door. The teddy bear in the blazer and tie sat smiling smugly. I wanted to walk right up to it and pull the tie tight around its stupid little neck.

'I can't do this,' Laura whispered. Her eyes sought out mine. I tried to smile.

'Remember the clocks,' I said. I rolled my eyes insanely and mimed a grandfather clock gone wrong. 'Tock-tick. Tock-tick.'

'Dad's not coming, is he?' she asked. I put my hands on her shoulders and turned her around and started brushing her hair.

'He'll be trying,' I told her. God, how I hated that word. 'He said he would. And all the rest of us are here.' She wasn't listening again.

'I'm on!' called one of her teammates. 'See you in the winner's circle.' She grinned at Laura as she passed. My heart was pounding, stuck halfway up my throat so that it was choking me. How could Laura stand it?

'He's not coming,' she said. 'He doesn't love us ...' Her voice was a whispered wail.

'Don't get the two of them mixed up,' I told her fiercely. 'He does love you!'

'And you!' she said. She twisted, then held my arms, digging in her fingers. 'And you!' she insisted.

'I know,' I said. Did I? 'He's just lost track a little right now.' Where had those words come from? I sounded like some kind of prime-time TV talk show host, always fair, seeing both sides. A sudden no-blame-no-pain phil-osophy.

'Laura!' It was her coach. 'Laura! You're on.'

'Hell!' I grabbed a rubber band and pushed

her hair hastily into a ponytail. Then I pulled her against me and hugged. Her body felt cold and unyielding. Rigid again. 'Good luck,' I told her. 'Remember the clocks!'

Did she even hear me? She moved stiffly past and began to climb onto the nearest trampoline.

The sickening thudding had expanded right down my chest and into my stomach. I had to open my mouth to breathe. I turned and hurried back to Kate and Mum.

⁓

She stood on the trampoline, motionless, carved from marble.

'She looks so young.' Kate's voice was barely audible.

'Good luck.' Mum whispered the words across the crowds and the judges and the waiting trampolines to my sister.

I lifted a hand to wave. But Laura's eyes were fixed far away. On the doorway.

A bell rang. The start of the routine. In a few seconds, Laura would raise her arms and start the bounce to build her height, soaring through the air. Flying. Soon now. The time stretched. The crowd stilled into silence, waiting. Then lightly, gracefully, Laura's arms raised, and she gave a tiny jump and lifted her body into the air.

Bounce. Bounce. She slowly gained height. Arms pulling powerfully. Legs straight, toes perfect.

Bounce. Bounce. Bounce. She was at top height now. One jump pulled her a little off centre. She corrected on the next. My fingers dug into each palm.

Bounce. Bounce. Bounce. Any minute now her body would open into the first trick. The soaring layout somersault she loved doing.

Bounce. Bounce. Bounce. Any minute now ... Beside me, Kate shifted uneasily.

'Now!' I breathed to Laura. 'Go now!' Why didn't she start?

Bounce. Bounce. Bounce. Bands were tightening around my chest.

'You can do it,' I whispered. 'Come on, Laura. The layout. Do it now!'

Kate murmured something meaningless, a prayer, a plea.

Bounce. Bounce. Bounce.

The judges flicked quick glances at the coach. The crowd shifted restlessly, whispering to itself.

Bounce. Bounce. Bounce.

The blue and white uniform of the coach

had moved to stand by the trampoline. Other blue and white uniforms were standing up, silent and watching, shaking their heads.

Bounce. Bounce. Bounce.

'Laura,' breathed Kate. 'Oh, my darling ...' The judges were looking at one another now. One of them stood and walked over to the coach.

Bounce. Bounce. Bounce.

The crowd was murmuring more loudly now. Sadly, shifting uneasily. Slowly, the coach moved to stand in front of Laura, his hand raised in a stopping gesture. She didn't see him.

Bounce. Bounce. Bounce.

Her eyes were staring straight ahead. Fastened to the door.

Bounce. Bounce. Bounce.

'Laura!' His voice echoed across the gymnasium. 'Laura!'

Bounce. Bounce. Bounce.

And then suddenly, she stopped. She stood rigid on the mat, eyes still fixed to the door. Not speaking. Not moving. No one else moved either.

With a tiny cry of pain, Kate broke and ran for the trampoline.

Chapter 19

The gym must have been a warehouse at one time, for out in the parking lot you could still see old signs like 'Goods Delivery to Rear' and 'Keep Clear for Front Loaders.' Laura's fingers were cutting into mine, but she stood still and unmoving while Kate had three goes at unlocking the car.

'We'll soon be home,' Kate said quietly. I felt something in Laura stir, and instinctively I moved closer. Kate got the door open at last, and a rush of hot air spilled over us. No one moved.

A taxi was pulling into the parking lot, its wheels spinning.

'Hello!' Dad was leaping out of the car, shovelling money at the driver even before it stopped. 'Finished already? Time for congratulations, I bet!' He moved towards Laura, arms held out. She made a sudden move backwards, still clinging to my hand. Dad slowed, took in the faces and stillness of us all, and then he stopped a few metres away. 'What happened?' he asked. His voice was suddenly wary.

Laura raised her head and stared at him, but she didn't answer. She didn't even blink.

'She did not compete,' said Kate.

'Didn't compete?' Dad took a step. 'Did they disqualify her or something?'

'No,' said Mum. 'She chose not to compete.' Her voice was carefully neutral.

'Why?' Dad looked at Laura. Her eyes locked onto his. But she kept silent.

'We don't know,' said Kate at last. None of us had asked. All we had done was get Laura out of there as quickly as possible. Away from the curious looks and pitying stares of the audience, away from the other blue and white uniforms and clamouring questions, away from the coach with his matter-of-fact sympathy.

'It happens,' he had said. 'Don't let it worry you. Next time.' And Laura had kept the eerie stillness even as she moved with us to the door.

'What was it?' Kate had moved in front now, taking Laura's hands, speaking so softly. 'What did happen?' There were tears running down her cheeks, but she didn't brush them away. Laura turned her head, and slowly her eyes followed.

But they were unfocused, confused.

'I couldn't remember,' she whispered. 'I just couldn't remember ...'

'Remember what?' Kate whispered back. Her knuckles were white, but she held Laura's hands as if they were precious flowers, too easily bruised.

'The first trick.' Laura began to tremble. 'I couldn't remember where to start.'

'But you've been practising that routine for months!' cried Dad. 'How could you forget?' The shaking in Laura's body was growing, spreading itself to Kate. I came in closer still and put my hands tightly against her shoulders. But suddenly Laura moved forward towards Dad, pushing us both away.

'Do you know the first trick?' she cried. 'Do you?'

'Er ...' Dad was startled. He'd never seen the routine. 'Er, was it the double back somersault?'

'Wrong!' said Laura. She took another step forwards. She and Dad were inches apart, eyes locked in the middle of the crowded parking lot. She was so much smaller than him, but he was the one backing away. 'I'll give you a hint, it was a somersault. But what kind?' Her voice was a command.

'Now, Laura ...' Dad was confused, hands

out in front, as if pleading with her, or trying to hold her off. 'Please. It's been a terrible week for us all. You're upset. And no wonder. The trouble over Tess has upset everything.'

Laura seemed to grow taller as we stood there. It wasn't possible.

'Don't you ever blame Tess again. Ever!' Her voice cut like electricity through the air. It was somehow shocking to hear. Was this really the peace-at-any-price sister I had always known?

'Please,' said Dad again. 'Let's get you home.' His hands made the pleading movement once more. He looked across to Kate. 'Let's go home,' he said again.

Kate made a movement towards their car, but Laura suddenly grabbed her arm, clinging fast.

'I won't go home!' she cried. 'I want to go home with Tess!' She reached out and grabbed me, too, pulling hard. Everyone started looking at everyone else.

'It's not right ... ' began Kate.

'I'm sure ...' Mum didn't know what to say.

'I want to go home with Tess!' Laura said again. You felt as if she would stand immobile in the centre of the parking lot until her want came true.

'Now Laura,' Dad said. He stopped, cleared

his throat, and began again. 'Laura, come home with us. You need your parents at a time like this.' He should never have said that. Laura turned and fixed huge, terrible eyes on his face.

'I needed you an hour ago!' she cried. 'Not now!' And turning, she walked stiff-legged and rigid towards Mum's car.

The rest of us just stood there. Then, with a shrug, Mum turned and started to follow.

'Come on,' she said. 'We may as well go back to our house. Have a cup of tea. Talk a bit.'

Hesitantly, everyone began to move. Dad too. But with a sudden movement of her hand, Kate stopped him.

'Not now,' she said. 'Not yet. We'll talk later.' And then, urging me in front of her, she too headed for Mum's car.

Laura and Kate, Mum and I. In all the years of our family I don't think we had ever been together in the same car.

Laura's body had started to shake again. Kate and I moved closer, sandwiching her in between, murmuring words that meant nothing and everything. When the tears started to flow, Kate wiped them away gently with her fingers.

As we pulled out of the parking lot, Dad

was still just standing there, looking after us. He seemed bewildered, lost. The big teddy bear rested against the side of the car where I had left it. As I watched he walked over and picked it up and buried his face in its fur.

Chapter 20

She was awake. I could hear it in her breathing in the darkness. I could even see faint movements of her body as she lay on the camp bed by my bed.

She and Kate had stayed all afternoon, the four of us sitting around the kitchen table, drinking cups of tea and resting our elbows in the crumbs left over from breakfast. We hadn't talked much about the trampolining. Early on, in words that kind of faded in and out, Laura had tried to explain: 'I must have done that routine hundreds of hundreds of times.' Kate had been sitting by her side, holding her hand, watching her closely. 'I never think about the tricks. Only about getting height, keeping my form, pointing my toes ...' She trailed off. There was silence for a long time. When she spoke again, all of us had to lean forward to hear. 'I didn't know where to begin,' she said at last. 'It was all just a blank ...' She looked across at Kate. 'What was the first trick?' she whispered.

'The layout,' Kate said gently. 'The layout back somersault.'

Laura was nodding, frowning. God, it must have been so hard for her.

'Oh yes.' She looked as if it hadn't quite slotted into her brain. 'And then came the ...?'

'Tuck back somersault.' Kate's voice would have lulled a tiny bird to sleep.

'Tuck back 'sault. Yes, tuck back.' She looked as if she were hearing the routine for the first time.

'I thought it was the straddle jump,' I said suddenly.

Mum shot a hard look at me. Laura was looking from Mum to me, confused. Kate looked frightened.

'It was the straddle jump. I'm sure of it,' I said. My heart was pounding.

'But the straddle jump is for height,' Laura began slowly. 'I used that before the big somersaults.' Something clicked. She lifted her head. Her eyes cleared. 'You idiot,' she said. 'It was the front 'sault next. In pike position. Then into the barani.' She knew now.

'Are you sure?' I was playing really dumb. The village idiot, scratching my head and crossing my eyes.

Laura was laughing and crying together. Her tears were dropping onto the table and sogging up the toast crumbs.

'I'm sure,' she said.

Later in the afternoon, Kate rang the coach at his home. He wanted to know how Laura was, what had happened. He had seen nerves freeze up competitors before and said it was nothing to worry about. 'Give her my love,' he said. He couldn't say anything for sure, but he promised to talk to the selection committee that week. 'Maybe we can get another trial for her,' he said. 'I surely hope so.'

Laura had nodded calmly when she heard the news. But you could see her clamping down hard on false hope. 'Maybe,' she said. And then she had gone on talking about some movie she thought we should go and see together.

~

When Kate left, Laura stayed.

It was late in the afternoon. Kate stood up, stretched, and pressed buttons on her mobile phone, calling a taxi.

'We must go,' she said. 'Michael will be waiting.'

'... you pull the string sideways ...' Laura was trying to teach me a cat's cradle when she heard Kate's voice. She suddenly jumped up, the stiffness back in her body, her face hard. 'I'm not going!' she said. 'I won't!' She shut her mouth suddenly and froze stock-still. She looked as if she had turned into a rock — as still and as immovable.

'But Laura!' For a moment Kate stood looking down at her, shocked. 'Please?' she begged. Laura didn't move, didn't speak. Did she even see Kate shake her head, pain written in her eyes? At last Kate sighed. 'Perhaps it's better this way.' Her voice trembled. 'Stay here with Tess.' She glanced at Mum, asking permission, and got a nod in return. Formalities and the careful politeness were long gone — she had almost taken that nod for granted. 'Michael and I have some talking to do. I'll come first thing in the morning.' She moved forward and put her arms around Laura. 'Bye, darling,' she whispered. And then she straightened and walked almost blindly out the door.

In the bedroom the darkness made sounds easier to hear. Enya was playing softly in the background; Mum put it on every night to lull me to sleep. Outside the window the huge old tea-tree creaked against the fence. And the waves washed up on the shore, blending in with the sounds of the wind — long, gentle, soothing.

Laura's breathing was quick and loud in the air, with tiny catches breaking in.

'Laura?' I didn't know what to say, so I used her name.

'Oh, Tess,' she said. 'What am I going to do? Everything is such a mess!' Her voice was a whispered wail.

'I know,' I said. It seemed as if it had been a mess forever. 'You should have told me,' I said. 'About the nightmares.' Why hadn't she?

'I couldn't,' she said. Her arms moved in the darkness, as if reaching into the air. 'If I had said anything ...' Her voice stopped. 'If you talk about them ...' She halted again until I heard her take a huge breath. 'If you say them aloud ... they may come true.' She let out the air with a rush.

'Dad needs us.' Maybe it was even true. He had stood in the parking lot all alone, holding tight to a teddy bear. 'He needs us more than we need him. We're all he has.' I'd never thought about it that way before. 'You should have told me,' I said again.

'Maybe.' Silence for so long I couldn't even

guess what she was thinking. Her breath came more evenly, or was it the sea, coming in, going out? Enya finished; a tiny click came as the CD shut off. A rustle in the camp bed as Laura adjusted her pillow. 'They hardly ever come,' she said at last. 'When you're there.'

I stared out the darkened window into the night. 'That's the dreamcatcher,' I said slowly. 'It traps your dreams too. The bad ones.'

Laura sat up. 'You think so?' she asked.

'Yes. I think so. Here.' I threw back the sheet and blanket and watched as Laura groped her way across to the bed. 'Come and see.' She slid in next to me. When we were younger we used to sneak into each other's bed all the time. It felt strange now. She took up so much more room. Her body was hard, full of muscle and sharp angles. I reached up to unhook the dreamcatcher, and then I put it into her hands. The feathers were sticking together from where I always touched them in the night. 'That's where the bad dreams are caught — in the web.' Her fingers were exploring the intricate net of cotton threads woven in the circle.

'Does it really work?' she said. 'Really?' Her fingers stroked the tiny stones knotted in the web.

'They'll be there,' I told her. 'All the bad

dreams, trapped in the threads.' Dad in the parking lot, looking so lost and alone. Laura standing, carved with fear and longing, watching the gym door. The breakers far out at the mouth of the bay, pounding and pulling me under. 'When the sun comes through the window each morning, the light burns them away.'

'Are you sure?'

'I'm sure.' I took the dreamcatcher from her and hung it back over the bed. 'Only the good dreams get through.'

Hidden by the night, the dreamcatcher swayed. Laura's body seemed softer now, less fierce. She curled it into mine, and it no longer seemed crowded in the bed. Slowly her breath lengthened, moving in and out, in and out, in time with the sea. At last mine did too.

Chapter 21

It hadn't rained for over a week, and any water left in the soil had been almost instantly dried by the wind. That meant more lugging of buckets to the plants above Whale Bay.

Laura and I waited until late afternoon, when the sun had lost its sting. It was cooler for us, better for the plants too.

'Do we have to water all these?' She looked around at the whole plantation and shook her head. 'All of them?'

'Er ... maybe just the small ones. The bigger plants can probably do without this week.' I didn't want to lose her right at the start. There were a heck of a lot of them. But I hadn't dared ring up the other Green Guerrillas and ask for help; that would have been pushing our luck.

'We should have made both our mums come and help,' said Laura. Kate had been coming and going all day. She and Mum were into about their seventh coffee and conversation. 'If I'd known there were this many plants, I'd have dragged Mum out by both arms.'

'I asked them twice already.' Mum and Kate had been welded to the kitchen table. 'Come on, get moving.' I led her over to the tap and started filling buckets. My muscles were stiff already, as if they knew what was coming.

For over an hour we filled, heaved, lugged, and poured. Why could I never manage to carry a bucket without bumping it on my leg and spilling at least a third on the way? The plants nearest the tap always got plenty of free water.

'Do you do this every Sunday?' Laura was panting. There were red marks from the bucket on her legs too.

'Not always.' I rubbed flies and sweat off my face. 'In the winter it rained heaps. We hardly had to do anything then.'

'And I always thought you just lazed around here. You know, lay on the beach, swam all day — ' She stopped abruptly. 'Sorry,' she said. 'I forgot about the swimming.' She knew I never went near the water now.

I concentrated on trickling water onto the thirstiest plants. She was waiting for me by the tap when I came back.

'Is that what happened to you?' she said. 'Yesterday at the gym. Is that what happened with your swimming?'

'Leave it, Laura.' Not this again. Why did she always go back to the swimming? I turned the tap on loudly.

'Tess!' Her voice was a tiny wail. 'Tess, I need to know. Yesterday. Is that what happened?'

The bucket was full. I turned the tap off and straightened to face her. 'There was nothing like that. Nothing sudden.' I cleared my throat and tried to make my voice less harsh. 'It was just that one day I figured out there was no fun in winning anymore. No satisfaction even. It only felt empty.' It was said at last. I waited. Silence for so long I couldn't even guess what she was thinking. I turned and lugged water to the farthest plants. Laura hadn't moved when I got back. But she didn't look upset — maybe puzzled, that's all.

'Don't you ever get tired of it?' I asked abruptly. 'All that training? All the competitions?' I had to know. I had to ask.

'No.' She looked at me curiously. 'I like all that. It's fun. Especially the competitions.' Even just talking about it you could hear the eagerness in her voice.

'You're serious, aren't you?' Why had I never realised that before? It seemed obvious now. But I'd always judged her by me, by the way I'd felt.

'Oh yes,' she said. 'I like to compete. I love to win.' She gave a tiny half laugh. 'When I remember the set, that is.'

'You'll remember,' I told her. 'With or without Dad there.'

She gave a small shrug, watching seagulls fly far out over the bay. 'Maybe,' she said.

'You will, Laura!' I said. 'You will!' She heard the urgency in my voice and looked back to me. Slowly she nodded.

'I will,' she promised.

'And you'll keep on going?' But I knew the answer now. Saw it in the proud lift of her head, in the small strong rows of muscles running the length of her body.

'Oh yes.' There was utter certainty in her voice. She thought for a moment, the silence stretching. 'I guess we really are different after all,' she said at last. I nodded, a slow smile starting from nowhere. We were different. It was a relief, a wonderful feeling of freedom. The smile spread, making me want to laugh, to shout, to fly. Different. I had never really known how much until today.

Several hundred flies on my back were still hitching a free ride to nowhere when I came back with the final empty bucket. Finished at last.

'It's beautiful.' Laura was shading her eyes, gazing across to Whale Bay while I threw the bucket onto the grass and tried to get the worst of the kinks out of my back. 'I wish I could come here more often,' she added.

'Maybe you can.' I thought of Kate and Mum talking, planning, laughing over the kitchen table. 'Things are changing, that's for sure.'

'You think it's possible?' There was real yearning in her voice. 'It's so perfect here.'

'Well, not always.' I had to be fair. 'There are disadvantages here too.' I stretched out on the grass and began pulling up tiny boneseed weeds around our feet.

'Like what?' she demanded. 'Name three!'

'Uhm ... well, when you hang your clothes on the line, they always dry salty. From the sea air.'

'Go on.' She was half laughing, half serious.

'And if you want to see a movie or get a

video or even buy a new pair of socks, you have to go all the way into town.' It was twenty minutes away by car.

'That's two,' she said.

'And, er ...' I thought hard. 'Sometimes I miss my friends and the rest of the family. Even you once or twice.' I couldn't tell her how much.

She laughed and threw a handful of sand and dirt at me. It stuck to the sweat all over. 'Next weekend,' she said, 'will you take me down to Whale Bay?' Here she was, the first visit in years, and she was already planning next weekend here too. I wondered if we would manage it. 'I want to go swimming,' she said. 'Can you jump off that big rock at high tide?' She was looking at the bay again.

'No.' I found a tiny tea-tree seedling in among the grass and absently trickled the last of the water from a bucket onto it. 'There aren't any rocks in Whale Bay.'

'What's that one then?' She was sitting up straight, pointing. I followed her gaze, and slowly I felt myself stand, my feet moving to the edge of the cliff. I didn't want to look; a sickening, horrible dread was forming. Whale Bay had no rocks. So what was that huge, dark shape right in the centre of the sand?

My feet were moving down the path, stumbling over sharp stones and rubble. I tripped, reached out a hand, started running. Laura was somewhere behind, running too. Something was choking me — I wanted to throw up. There were no rocks in Whale Bay. Down, stumble, down. Where was the air to breathe? My feet hit the bottom; I was still moving, still running across the sand. The rock grew bigger before me, lying sideways just out of the water. But there were no rocks in Whale Bay ...

'No!' I cried. 'No!' I flung myself across the sand. The shape was in front of me now, forcing me to stop. It spread, three times my length, dark and unmoving. As still as a rock.

But there were no rocks in Whale Bay.

Only a whale.

Chapter 22

It was alive. I knew it, even before I saw the great sides move inward. I heard the breath coming out in one sharp hissing blow. A dark eye looked into mine — did it show hope — or fear? Across the face, a great sward of fishing net was tangled, cutting into the skin.

'Help me!' I cried to Laura. The body of the whale lay sideways to the shore, toppled onto one side, so close to the water one wave actually touched its side. I wrapped my arms around its tail and tried to pull. Laura was beside me, arms straining, pulling too. The skin of the whale felt harsh and dry, like rubber left too long in the sun, and somehow frightening to touch.

'Pull!' I shouted. My feet dug into the sand. I could see all the muscles in Laura's arms stand out, straining. She was so strong, all that training, all those weights. Surely between us, we could move him.

'Pull!' I called again. We could drag it back to the sea. Of course we could. It was such a small way to the water.

No movement. No movement at all.

My feet were sinking deep into the sand, struggling to find a foothold. I felt the whale's dry skin tug against my own. I tightened my arms, bracing both feet against the betraying sand.

'This time,' I cried. 'Pull now!' If muscle wouldn't do it, willpower could. Laura's body was leaning hard backward, her muscles and face set. I heard blood thrumming in my ears.

We felt the tensing of the whale's muscles only as the huge tail half lifted into the air and then suddenly thrashed against the sand. *Whoomp!* We were flung back, stumbling in panic. God, it was so big, so strong! *Whoomp*. *Whoomp*. All the whale's body was heaving now, struggling against its own dead weight, which trapped it on the sand.

'Stop it!' I cried. Its tail lifted again. *Whoomp*. It thrashed against the sand. 'Stop! Don't!' How do you talk to a whale? I felt impossibly, terribly helpless.

Laura was on all fours in the water, struggling to breathe.

'It's no good,' she gasped, looking terrified. 'It's too big.'

I splashed into the sea beside her. 'It needs water!' Frantically I began scooping handfuls of sea and throwing them. The water made tiny dark drops against the whale's skin. Most of it fell short.

'The buckets,' said Laura. She was still panting for breath. 'They're at the plantation.' She ran towards the path. Before she got halfway across the sand, she had to drop to a walk, with a hand held against her chest.

'I'll go.' I took a step towards her. She shook her head, her breath coming more easily now, and kept on moving.

I felt like I was in some kind of demented egg-and-spoon race, splashing into the sea, carrying handfuls of water up the shore, and then throwing them carefully against the dry skin of the whale. The net lay meshed against its face. I wanted to take it, tear it away, as if it were the net that was holding the great animal on the shore. But I kept on carrying precious handfuls of wetness.

Laura was running back across the beach, carrying the buckets. She dipped the first one into the sea and flung a great rush of water onto the whale's skin. It tensed, the tail moved again in a tiny thump, and then it lay still. Another bucket of water. And another. Whole patches of its hide grew wet, glistening almost black. We kept scooping water.

A tiny whistling sound came into the air, too small surely to have come from the whale. Its whole hide was wet now, gleaming and smooth. I moved to touch its head. Through the net, one large dark eye watched me.

'The net,' said Laura. 'Can you get it off?'

Carefully I took hold of the nylon. It was tangled in great knotted layers in its mouth, mashed among the teeth. Flesh showed bright red against the pink of its gum where the strands had sawn and cut.

'Easy now,' I crooned. 'Let me help you. Easy now.' My fingers pulled at a square and locked into each side, yanking and straining.

'How could it see with that there?' asked Laura. 'How could it swim?'

I shook my head, fingers still pulling. 'It couldn't. They work on sonar or something. It must have panicked and come too close to shore. And got beached.' There were other images too. I tried to block them. They kept coming — the whale swimming endlessly, its great jaws tangled shut, growing hungry, slowly starving, each day becoming weaker and more confused until ... I didn't say anything to Laura. One nightmare at a time was enough.

The nylon had scored deep grooves into my fingers. I could feel the bruising start.

'Give up,' said Laura. 'We'll have to cut it off.' I tried one last stretch and pull. More pain, sharper this time. Blood flowed from several fingers. I shook my head. The loops were made to withstand sharks in a frenzy. I had no hope.

We went back to carrying water. Scoop, step, walk, splash. Each time we filled the buckets they seemed to grow heavier. Each step up the beach seemed longer. We had fallen into a heavy slog of scooping buckets, painfully slow and steady. The whale had not moved again, but you could hear the harsh hiss each time it blew out air.

'The tide's going out,' said Laura. Her words sounded ominous. I looked across to the shore-line, panting. She was right; the water was far-ther from the whale — and still retreating. The tide was going out — what did that mean? I struggled to think clearly. I was supposed to be the leader, the organiser, the one with all the bright ideas. Reluctantly, I figured it out.

'High tide is in the morning,' I said at last.

'We'll be here all night.'

Laura put down her bucket. 'We need help,' she said. 'I'm going to get Mum and Margot. They'll be worried.'

How long had we been there? I stopped, too, and let my own bucket drop. 'Wait,' I said. I needed more time to think. Planning — wasn't that what I'd always prided myself on? Think then! Plan! Get organised. 'Tell them to ring the council or the Maritime Museum,' I said. 'And ring Colin and Toni and Jacob and get them to come down. No, not Toni, she's been grounded.' I shook my head, trying to clear it. Think, for God's sake! 'And bring towels ... no, blankets, we can wet them. And some food.' Laura was already setting off towards the path. 'And some big scissors!' She waved without looking back and kept on walking.

The body of the stranded whale gleamed in the lowering sun. Water from the buckets ran in tiny streams down the sand — back into the sea. I stood for a moment, watching. Then I moved to sit in front of the dark blunt head.

'The tide is going out,' I told him. 'It's going to be a long night.'

A seagull settled on the shore, ruffled its wings, and stood with one leg up. It looked at the curved flanks of the whale thoughtfully.

'Go away.' I picked up a handful of sand and threw it. 'Shoo!' It spread its wings haughtily and flapped away.

'In the morning,' I told the whale, 'the tide will come in. The water will come back.' I reached out and touched the face tentatively. His mouth curled upward like it was smiling, but the eyes, the eyes ... The net scratched against my skin.

My hands slowly stroked against his face. There was a smell of salt and sea. Only a few hours ago, he had been swimming free out in the great ocean. He had felt the waves, seen kelp move in the currents. And then he had found the net ...

'I'm sorry.' It was like an apology from the whole human race. 'So very sorry.'

The patient eyes of the whale stared at me, waiting.

Chapter 23

They came in a rush, dead heating down the path and stumbling onto the beach — Mum and Laura with armfuls of tartan blankets and towels; Colin and Ian, his dad, carrying more blankets and buckets; and Kate, ever practical, with roughly cut sandwiches in a huge plastic bag with her mobile phone balancing on top. They had taken forever.

'Tess! Oh, Tess,' said Mum. But she was looking at the whale. His breath hissed in a sharp blow, one eye following the people as they spilled onto the beach. 'Oh, my God,' whispered Mum. She seemed aghast at his size — at the enormity of the task that faced us all.

'Soak those blankets in the sea,' said Ian. 'Lay them on top of the poor fella. We'll have to keep him wet all night.' Laura and Mum were rolling up their shorts, wading out into the waves, where they dunked the blankets. Colin grabbed the ends as they flung them over the whale, straightening them. The tartan covered vast areas of skin. We scooped buckets and poured water, wetting the blankets even further. Ian moved to the side of the whale and sat down in the sand, his back propped firmly against the dark flanks. 'Now let's get him upright. Stop the muscles cramping.' He motioned for us to help, waiting until we had all followed, wedging our feet firmly in the sand. He seemed to know exactly what to do. 'That's right. Ready? Now push, all together now.' Feet scrabbled in sand, I gritted my teeth, heard Colin grunt. Through the blanket, my shoulders heaved against the flanks of the whale while my feet dug great furrows in the sand. 'Strongly now. Keep pushing.' I felt something move, the weight lighten. Then slowly, surely, the body of the whale rolled and settled in a new position on the sand, upright now.

'He'll be more comfortable this way,' said Colin, wiping sweat. I nodded. I remembered now. He and his dad had been here years ago when the great mass of whales had been stranded and died — and given Whale Bay its name. Colin told me they had worked for two days without a break, digging and bucketing and hoping. Only three of the pilot whales had been saved. The rest had died in agony.

Neighbourhood punks had gathered on the point with their air rifles and beer cans and used the bodies for target practice.

'Right. Now the rest of us can start digging.' Colin's dad had one of those calm voices that stayed soft all the time.

'Dig where?' I asked. 'Why?' I saw Kate and Laura thinking the same thing.

'Around the flippers,' he said. He didn't seem put out at being asked dumb questions. 'Without the water to cool him, he'll overheat. Whales lose excess heat through their flippers. So we make a pool around each flipper to keep them wet.'

'Whales can breathe on land,' said Colin. 'It's the heat that kills them.'

Through the damp cloth of my T-shirt, I felt the sun's rays, hot and drying. I wiped sweat, feeling sick. If I was hot, what must the whale be feeling? It was terrible to think he was baking, boiling, dying here under the sun, even as we stood around talking.

I dropped down on my knees. 'Come on!' I cried. 'We have to hurry.' I started heaving sand furiously.

'Slowly now.' I felt a hand on my shoulder from Mum.

'We've a long haul in front of us,' Ian said. How could they be so calm? The whale blew air again, a hard, sharp burst. It was so hot. We had to hurry! One of the huge flippers lay crushed against its side. Ian knelt beside me and gently straightened it out. 'Just take it steady,' he said. 'It works better that way.' I nodded, clamped down hard on the panic, and kept on scooping.

Mum and Laura went back to carting buckets, tipping the water over the blankets, their feet stumbling in the holes we had dug.

'Don't get water near his blowhole. That's how he breathes,' said Colin. He was next to me, digging too. Kate was sitting on the sand, punching numbers on the phone and getting no answers.

'Have you tried the Department of Environment and Land Management?' asked Mum.

'Yes,' she said wearily. 'And Conservation and Natural Resources. It's Sunday night. Who would be working now?'

'Try the Marine Discovery Centre,' Ian suggested. 'There must be someone who can help.' Kate sighed and began punching numbers again.

Water was gathering in a pool at the bottom of my hole, soaking the sand and making it heavy. I trickled some of the water over the flippers. My arms were trembling, work and worry combining.

'Move along a bit,' said Colin. He hadn't stopped. But then he hadn't been hauling buckets all afternoon either. I could hear blood thumping through my ears continuously now. 'Make the hole longer out here,' said Colin. 'It'll be more comfortable for his flippers.'

I was so tired Colin had to wait while I figured out how to get my legs to obey. Scoop and throw, scoop and throw. The hole was deep now, water seeping in from all sides. Reaching out, Colin and I settled the great flipper carefully in the hole's centre.

'I'll take over if you like.' Max, Jacob's father, was kneeling beside me. Behind him, Toni and Jacob stood, hesitating before the great face of the whale. There were tears in Toni's eyes. I nodded at Max and tried to mutter some thanks. He sat next to Colin and cupped water over the flipper. I managed to totter back about three steps before I sank onto the sand for a rest.

'I thought you were grounded for a month,' I finally got out to Toni.

'I was,' she said. 'But your mum got on the phone to mine and, well, here I am.' I nodded.

I could almost hear Mum, using the special voice she reserved for important clients, charming and persuasive. Toni's mum would have to stay at home; she had the twins to look after and no one to help out. But she had let Toni come.

'He's so beautiful,' murmured Toni. Her eyes hadn't left the whale. 'So big.'

'Incredible.' There was awe in Jacob's voice. Through the tangled pile of netting the whale seemed to be watching us.

'Did you bring any scissors?' I asked. 'We have to get that net off somehow.'

'Here,' said Toni. 'Is that what they were for?' She moved closer to the whale's head and hesitantly picked up a bit of loose net. She seemed scared to touch him. The scissors slowly snipped once, twice. 'It's really tangled,' she said. 'How did it happen?'

'It's fishing net.' Jacob's teeth were clenched, his voice bitter. In his house high above Break-sea, his bedroom faced directly onto the sea. He spent so many hours watching, lying on his bed, seeing its changing faces. His room was filled with books about the creatures that grew and swam and floated under that surface. 'Fishing net.' He bit out the words again. 'When they get too worn, fishermen just cut them free and dump them overboard.' There was silence for a moment, then he spelled it out for her. 'Dolphins and whales are curious. They like to play with things they don't understand. Bloody fishermen.' His face was twisted, and his mouth kept moving, although no more words came out.

'Isn't that illegal?' I asked. Surely it must be. So many laws. Don't jaywalk, don't duck out of school, don't trespass on Comcor's smokestack. All made for protecting humans. How many laws were made to protect animals?

'It wouldn't matter anyway.' Jacob shrugged, face taut. 'Some people never think …'

Kate had given up on the phone and joined Mum and Laura in pouring more water over the whale. Jacob stood stiffly and moved towards Colin.

'My turn now,' he said and started digging.

Two pools of water were filling, flowing under the whale's flippers. Ian and Max were carefully walking around the whale, lifting blankets, checking for any injuries.

'A few scrapes under here.'

'This side's fine.'

I knelt close to the whale's head and untangled net while Toni snipped and cut.

'We're trying to help,' I whispered. 'Hold on. We can help.'

'Poor thing,' said Toni. 'The poor, poor thing.' She brushed angrily at more tears and kept on cutting. Laura came with a bucket and gently poured water over the whale's head, carefully avoiding his blowhole.

'Can he hear us?' she asked.

I spread the water over the glistening forehead. 'I don't know,' I said, watching his eyes. 'I think so.'

The whale was almost free of the net. Only the last bits, wound tightly around the teeth, remained.

'Would you open wider now?' Toni nudged against the whale's face, and the great mouth moved. Her hands worked carefully among the pointed teeth, untangling net, fear forgotten. I took over the scissors, cutting carefully. The whale could have so easily closed his mouth, crushing fingers and bone, but we didn't pause. Somehow we knew he wouldn't.

'Nearly there,' said Toni. She reached far back, untangling by feel. 'Done!' she said at last and threw the last piece of net onto the pile.

It was easier to look at the whale now, to meet his eyes. I stroked the beautiful blunt head. 'Tomorrow,' I promised him. 'Tomorrow the tide will come back. Then you'll be swimming far out in your sea again. Back where you belong.' His skin felt like wet rubber, glistening. 'Tomorrow,' I promised and kept on stroking.

The loud ring of the mobile phone sounded frightening, almost alien against the sounds of the sea. Mum jumped, slopping water over her shorts. Kate shook her head, puzzled, and moved up the shore. 'Might be the council,' she said, sounding hopeful. 'I left a message.' She picked up the phone.

'Kate, where the hell are you?' Everyone heard the voice. Laura and I looked at each other. It was Dad.

'I'm at the beach.' Kate's voice was calm. Then suddenly her face changed. 'Oh,' she cried. 'The mayoral ball!' She had forgotten. Tonight she and Dad were supposed to be wearing their best glad rags, tucking into all those tiny bits of food that cost a fortune, and trying not to trip over each other's toes on the dance floor. She glanced down at her drenched shorts, met Mum's eye, and grinned ruefully. 'No, I'm not ready for the ball,' she said. Her voice grew firmer. 'I won't be coming to the ball.' We didn't hear what Dad said. Kate had pressed the phone closer to her ear, blocking his words.

'There's a whale, beached near Margot's place,' she said into the phone. 'We can't leave it.' Silence as she pressed the phone hard against her head. What was Dad saying?

'Let them be disappointed,' she said. Mum looked down, suddenly busy making furrows in the sand. Jacob's dad picked up a spare bucket and dipped it into the sea. Kate was speaking again, not seeing us, her eyes focused on the distance, far out to sea.

'You come here,' she said. 'We could do with some more help.'

'Do you think he will?' Laura whispered to me.

'Fat chance,' I muttered. Her face fell. I would have thought she'd have been glad.

'Michael!' Kate's voice rang out clearly. I felt the hairs down my neck and back prickle. 'Remember what we said.' In the sudden silence, each word echoed in the air like a warning. For a moment she listened, watching the sea, her face set. Then she gave a tiny nod, as if in confirmation, and hung up the phone. She looked at Laura and me. We waited.

'He's coming,' she said.

Chapter 24

A sunset of orange, red and gold was etching itself across the sky. Waves broke with a soft rush onto the sand.

Onshore, the great whale lay, alien and eerie, swathed in tartan blankets.

Down the path a man came, walking in suit and tie. In his hands two cheap plastic bags swung bulging. He looked alien, too, lost.

'Dad!' Laura cried and raced across the sand. He dropped the heavy bags and knelt down as she reached him, arms wide.

'Laura,' he said. 'My Laura.' And he held her.

No one else moved.

'I knew he would come!' Laura swung around to me. 'I knew!'

One of the bags had split when it dropped. Square cardboard juice boxes and apples had splayed over the sand. We all watched as Dad bent clumsily to pick them up. Kate moved forward, as if her legs were weighed down by concrete.

'Hello, Michael,' she said.

'I brought you some food.' Dad's voice was hesitant. 'I thought perhaps you might need something.' He was holding out the split bag half filled with apples and covered with sand. For some reason, the thought of him pushing a supermarket cart, loading it with drinks and crackers and fruit, made my eyes sting hotly.

'Come and see him!' Laura was tugging at his arm. 'The whale.' As if Dad could miss it on that tiny beach. But he let her lead him to its great head, where I was still kneeling, slowly tipping water from a bucket down his skin. 'Isn't he beautiful?' she asked.

Somehow Dad's eyes had locked onto mine.

'Are you all right, Tess?' he asked. I nodded. I couldn't find any words.

'You must be Tess's father.' Ian had come up, then Jacob and his father, and Toni and Colin, all talking and offering handshakes and names. One wide, dark eye of the whale followed their movements, watching. Even Mum came, a half smile in place as she regarded him curiously.

'Glad you could come, Michael.' She shook his hand. Her voice was as casual as if they were old friends at a dinner party. 'I hope you're not too fond of that suit.' And with a grin, she looped the handle of a bucket over his arm.

~

We were back to digging again. In the pools around the flippers, water lapped at the sides, pulling sand inward. We scooped it out time after time. The whale's skin was dark black now, wet and gleaming. Beneath his throat were white markings in some sort of strange anchor shape. Often, I stopped and rested my hands against his hot flanks.

'We'll save him,' said Colin. 'He'll be just fine.' I smiled tiredly at him.

'How's your face?' I asked. He reached up a hand to touch where the banner had scored across. Dark rain cloud colours had spread across one side of his face, with the whip mark itself making a deeper rainbow down the middle. It looked sore.

'Getting better,' he said. He would never mention pain.

'So you're the one who nearly pushed my son off the tower!' Colin's dad had wandered near.

'Er ...' I started to back off. 'Not quite,' I managed. Was he still mad about that? In the growing darkness, I saw Dad stop pouring water, listening in.

'He's teasing,' said Colin. His dad laughed and reached forward to ruffle my hair.

'At least you brought him safely home again,' he said. God, Colin was lucky to have him.

Laura and Dad were pouring water, side by side. Dad had taken off his suit jacket and tie as well as his shoes. His feet seemed white and fragile as they moved across the sand. The sun was long gone. The night air was cooling the sand. Kate was giving out the sandwiches she'd brought and the packets of drinks. I moved to sit by the side of the whale again as I ate.

'Soon,' I whispered to him. 'High tide will be coming soon. Just the other side of night.' One eye slowly blinked at me. Had he understood? The darkness was closing all around.

'It's getting cold.' Laura had come up. She was taking huge bites out of her sandwich, barely chewing before she swallowed.

'Get a towel,' I said. 'Some of them are still dry.'

'Later.' She looked across to where Dad was still bailing water. 'You should talk to him, you know.'

'About what?' It had all been said many times before. The words rang around and around in my head. 'You're never here! You never listen!

You'll never understand!' I was so tired of all the fights and bitter words.

'He does love us. Really he does.' Who was she trying to convince? 'You said yourself he needed us.'

'It's different for you.' It was, wasn't it? I looked across to where Dad was talking to Jacob and his father. He was crouched down on the sand, listening as they explained how to dig out the sand around the whale's flippers. There was a chance for Laura. But for me?

'Why?' she insisted. 'Why is it different?'

'I'm so much older.' I could hardly understand it myself. Too old to believe in fairy tales and happy endings. I knew now that sometimes the cavalry came over the hill just a little too late.

I stood up and hijacked a sandwich off Kate as she passed. She grinned and gave me a hug and kept on moving. Laura was still waiting for me, chewing thoughtfully.

'Marine ecologists,' she said after a pause, 'need to be good swimmers.'

I had thought of that, often. 'I can swim,' I said quickly. 'You know that.'

'Can you?' she asked. I looked over the sand to the water beyond. It gleamed dark and sinister in the night. I shivered.

'It's a long time ahead,' I said. 'In the future.'

She chewed, head tilted to one side, considering. A tiny breeze had come up, making both of us cold now. 'I know what to get you for your birthday,' she said at last. Her tone told me she was leading up to something.

'What?' I asked. In the darkness it was hard to tell if she was serious or not. But Laura was always serious.

She paused, holding on to the moment, and finally let the words go. 'Water wings,' she said, and bits of sandwich sprayed everywhere as she laughed.

'And *I've* got a book for *you*.' I wasn't going to let her get away with that. 'Try *How to Improve Your Memory in Twenty-one Days*.'

We both cracked up, laughing.

The sound made the whale give a loud blow, then a tiny chirping sound came, faint in the air between us. We looked at him. The corners of his mouth were turned permanently upward, so that he looked like he was smiling. Even when the net had cut deep into his mouth, he had looked like that. I stroked the blunt mound of his forehead. It felt like gleaming rubber tugging gently at my skin.

The chirping sound came again. In the darkness, I saw Laura looking puzzled. 'Can he understand?' Her eyes watched his face with wonder. I rested my own face against the smooth skin. He smelled of salt and of sea stretching far into the distance.

'I don't know,' I said. 'Anything is possible.'

'They're out there, you know.' She was serious now for sure.

'Who?' I looked at her curiously.

'All of them. The rest of the whales.'

'Other whales?' I had never thought about that. 'Are you sure?'

'Oh yes. I saw them at sunset. You could see their dorsal fins against the waves.'

I looked out at the water. The rush of the breakers foaming far out at the mouth of the bay gleamed white. The rest was darkness, impossible to see.

'It must be his pod,' I said slowly. 'They always swim in groups.' Where had I learned that?

Laura nodded. 'They're still there,' she said. She turned and scanned the sea, eyes as distant as the horizon. She seemed to have grown so tall, so old somehow. 'They're waiting for him.' Her voice cut clearly across the night, sure and strong. 'They know.'

Chapter 25

The edges of the towel were sopping wet. It was Colin's and my turn with the buckets. I pulled the towel tighter around me, pouring water and wondering if I would be warmer without it.

'I think the tide has turned,' Colin said. 'It's coming closer now.' I hoped he was right. Surely he was right. It was the nadir of the night, cold and black, and we were all exhausted. Were the waves really farther up the shore? In the darkness it was so hard to think straight.

Mum and Kate were making trips up the long, dark path to home, collecting more food and clothing and towels. They had promised to bring back more dry jackets and jeans in their next trip. All our blankets were draped over the whale to keep it wet.

'... I hear Tasmania's nice for a holiday,'

Kate was saying. They hadn't stopped talking all night. 'Not too expensive either.'

'I've got relatives there.' Mum was starting up the path. They were on their third or fourth trip now. 'Near Hobart.'

'So have I!'

'Maybe we could go together!' Their laughter came back down the path. They sounded like school kids planning a midnight feast.

Toni, Jacob, and his dad were resting their hands against the whale, rocking him gently from side to side. The cramps had started now. Trapped by his own weight, the great muscles of the whale were tightening, fighting one another. Even if we got the whale back into the sea, we would have to stand in the water, holding on to him until the spasms eased and he was strong enough to swim free.

'... police brought back my rope,' Max was saying. 'Nice of them.' They must have been talking about the Comcor tower. It had been his rope we'd used.

'... seemed such a great idea.' That was Jacob's voice.

'... the seal pup campaign was better.' Toni speaking now.

'Seal pups?' Jacob's dad didn't know about that. Toni and her big mouth. 'What was the seal pup campaign?'

I dipped the bucket into the sea and came back, trudging and shivering. They were smiling now, teeth gleaming in the darkness. Max was chuckling. 'You didn't!' he was saying. 'Not the mayor! You didn't!'

~

The whale was wet all over once more. Colin and I stopped bucketing. I took the last pail and poured it gently over the whale's head.

'There,' I murmured. 'Does that feel better?' I stroked his sides, under the blankets. They were smooth and shiny. The tiny chirping sound came again. He was making it more often now. Was he talking to me? Or was he trying to send out messages to the whales who waited for him past the breakers, far out at the mouth of the bay?

Colin had joined his dad, sitting at the edge of the shore, feet close to the white foam of the water. In the quiet, the sound of the waves was loud. The water in the bay gleamed black and oily, secrets lurking below.

'The fishing is better over in Squire's Bay,'

Ian was murmuring. 'We could take the dinghy there.'

'Do the early morning shift,' agreed Colin. 'Start about four o'clock in the morning. Pack a picnic breakfast.'

'. . . remember the four-pounder we landed over there?'

'Boxing Day. I remember. And you had a Christmas hangover.'

'We've never done that, have we, Tess? Gone fishing together?' Dad's voice, right next to me. God, he made me jump. Where had he come from?

'No,' I said. Slowly I stroked the whale's sides. 'You weren't that kind of father.' What kind of father had he been? He had chaired meetings, debating the importance of educational reforms — while I did my homework alone. He had listened and nodded at endless meetings about equal opportunity and child care while Kate and Mum drove me back and forth to the weekly changeovers year after year. He had said his family came first with him, always. He had never been home.

'We should do it one day.' Without his public speaking tone, Dad's voice had little shakes in it. 'Borrow some rods, go fishing together.'

'No.' I shook my head slowly. 'I don't like fishing.'

We had never gone fishing. Never worked on a vegetable patch together. He had gone to only one school play the whole time I'd been at school.

'We could try?' he said. 'Please, Tess.'

I'd been all of seven years old. He had sat in the front row of the school hall with an idiotic grin all over his face while I played a fairy stuck up a tree.

'I couldn't put a worm on the hook,' I said.

'I could teach you.'

'They're still alive. The worms. I couldn't stick the barb through their body. It's not right.'

'Maybe we could go to the park then. Fly a kite or something.'

He had taken me to the park and helped me clamber over the seesaws and jungle gym and swings. He had clapped and clapped as I learned to swing myself back and forth on my own.

'Laura would like that,' I said. 'She's got a kite. Take her.' I was watching the white edges of the waves lapping against the shore.

'Kate told me …' He stopped. In the night, I heard him swallow. 'Kate said you want to go to Margot's, for a few months.'

'I'm thinking of it,' I said.

'Don't leave us, Tess.' It sounded strange, like a plea.

He had come home from work when I fell off the monkey bars in second grade. He had held me on his knees for three hours while I howled and they X-rayed my arm and put it in a cast.

'You won't miss me,' I said. 'You're never home anyway.'

'Things can change, Tess. I can change.' He reached over and picked up my hand. My fingers felt stiff and cold in his.

He had taken my hand and walked with me to the local shops to buy a red icy pole and blue bubble gum. He'd laughed when I'd tried to eat both of them together.

'It wouldn't work.' My voice came out harsh and croaky.

'I love you so much, Tess.'

I buried my face against the whale's smooth skin and shivered. Silence seemed to surround us all. What could I say? How long had I waited to hear those words. Now they had come. But too late. Far too late. All I wanted to do was cry.

The silence grew, stretched, went on into eternity. At last Dad moved.

'You're cold,' he said. 'Wait here.' He stood

up stiffly and moved into the darkness. When he came back he placed his suit coat over my shoulders.

'It'll get wrecked.' I forced the words out.

'It's not important,' he replied. He waited for a moment, trying to think of other words. 'Things could be different, Tess.' He rested a hand on my shoulders. 'If we make them.'

Could they?

He had thrown me up in the air when I was a toddler. And tickled my sides until I laughed and laughed and laughed.

Could they?

When I looked up at last, he was gone.

～

My face had been resting against the whale's for so long now. I was tired, just so tired. The suit coat prickled against my skin, but at least it kept me warm. The tiny mewing sound came, soft and gentle.

'Soon now,' I promised him. 'It will be morning soon.' Dawn and the high tide would come together. Slowly the water would grow deeper, flow in under the whale, soothing, caressing. With the sunrise, he would experience the first feelings of floating, of freedom. All we had to do was wait.

'Everything will be fine,' I whispered, closing my eyes. I could talk to him more easily that way. 'When the water comes, you'll just float away free. We're here. We'll help. Everyone is here. Colin's dad knows just what to do. Jacob's dad too. We love you. We'll help you. Everything will be fine. Colin's dad's here. Everything's fine. Dad's here ...'

I could hear the great whale's heartbeat as I slept.

Chapter 26

It was the dream again. Far out from shore I was swimming, hands slicing the water, body strong, free. Swimming and swimming while the shore got farther and farther away. Dad would be sitting onshore. Soon, I'll call out to him — but he won't come, he never comes into the water. Soon, too, my arms will grow heavy and my chest will start to burn, craving air.

Still swimming. I feel the pull of the rip, strong, silent, carrying me with it. The waves grow larger, rushing against my body, cold and numbing. It must be the breakers at the mouth of the bay. I lift my head. White water rushes against my face. I suck in a breath and dive deep below the waves, deep, deep, deep. The dreamcatcher will stop the dream soon, but strangely I don't want it to. Why aren't my arms heavy now? Down, down I swim, under the waves, under the water, my whole body light and free. Down, down, down.

This wasn't the way the dream went. Down, down, down. Sounds came to me. 'Chirrup.' The whale was swimming with me now, pushing me up. 'Chirrup.' My whale.

'Go down!' I cried. 'I don't want to go back!'

'Chirrup. Chirrup.' The whale kept pushing.

Someone was squeezing me on the shoulder; a voice was using my name.

'Move back now, Tess. He's feeling the water.'

My feet were sunk in water and freezing cold. My face made a long sticking noise as I lifted it from the whale's skin.

'Move back, Tess. He's getting restless. You might get hurt.'

Hurt me? My whale wouldn't hurt me. Hands were pulling me back. Everything was gray light and foaming water and the sound of the whale, chirruping and calling again and again.

The tide had come in.

'Here.' Jacob was stumbling and yawning and holding out a wet suit. 'Get this on.'

'Wet suits?' Dad's voice was quiet as he

made the words a question. He was leaning against the flanks of the whale, holding him upright. He looked like he'd slept standing that way.

'We'll need them.' Colin was there too. 'For when the whale starts to float.'

'Why?' asked Dad. 'Won't he just swim away?'

Hadn't anybody told him? Colin just shook his head. 'It won't be over that soon,' he said quietly. 'We'll have to rock him. Rock him in the water until his muscles stop cramping.'

It was cold light; dawn hadn't come yet. My legs were icy numb, threatening to buckle. I hunkered deeper into Dad's suit coat, smelling warmth and wool and the faint tang of the shaving soap he always used. Memories.

'I'm freezing,' said Toni. She was already in a wet suit. It was old and way too huge. Her mum's probably. Her mum would be awake now, waiting for her to come home. Ever since Toni's dad had left years ago, her mum had spent a lot of time waiting and worrying. But she had still let Toni come.

'We'll turn him now,' Ian called. The time! The tide! I threw off Dad's coat and struggled into my wet suit. Toni and Jacob had already pulled the blankets from the whale's back and were pushing long folds of them against his flanks.

'Roll him.' Ian and Dad had their shoulders against the whale, rolling him over sand and blanket. I ran to help Colin scrabbling on the other side, heaving and pulling bits of tartan through.

'Right. Got it.' Beneath the head and the tail, the blankets would make a sling to lever the whale around.

'Everyone grab hold.' We would turn him to face the ocean — before the waves came in and washed him sideways and pushed him farther into the sand. Laura was beside me. Once before we had tried to move the whale — and failed. We had been alone then, just the two of us. We weren't trying to lift him, just swivel him around. It would be easy, simple ...

'Now!' I felt a grunt, a heave, and the sand scrunch and scrape against my feet. Tartan blanket strained against my hands. My feet were scrabbling to get a grip, moving backward. Moving, and the great bulk of the tail was moving too. Moving, moving ...

'That's it!' someone grunted. And the whale lay facing the water, just a metre from freedom. His eyes followed the motion of the waves. He made the small chirruping sound again. He knew. Laura sank to the sand with a sigh.

'Easy as a double back somersault with your eyes shut.' She grinned at me.

The waves were reaching higher up the shore. Once, twice, they touched the dark sides of the whale and ebbed slowly back.

'Get the trench made!' Ian's voice was suddenly loud. 'Let's get the water in.' He and Dad were on their knees, digging together to form a pathway from the whale to the sea. Water was surging up it. The waves made the sides cave in almost immediately. Mum and Kate waded in and started scooping out great handfuls of sand.

The whale's sides were wet now. Was it just the movement of the water, or was I really seeing small flickers of muscle quivering through his length?

The water rose with each wave and then subsided, lapping around him.

All of us were working on the trench, scooping frantically, scoring a deep trough to the sea. Water rushed in, churned, and slowly trickled back.

'Chirrup. Chirrup.' He was calling more loudly now. The water grew deeper. The sea was reaching out to him. The whale's great bulk was still trapped in the sand. But you felt that soon — with just a little bit more water — he could be free.

'Almost,' said Colin next to me. 'Almost.'

Just a little bit more water. Was the tide still coming in? Would it get higher? If he didn't make it out on this tide, we would never save him.

The whale's breath was coming in quick blows. His flippers were floating.

Soon. Soon. Just a bit more water.

The great whale's eyes flicked shut and then opened again. He was staring straight at me. His tail — it was moving, wasn't it?

Soon. Soon.

The trough was awash with waves.

'Now!' called Ian. He moved quickly to the head of the whale and grabbed hold of the blanket. Laura was there already. Mum and I grabbed the other side.

'Get the back blanket,' Colin cried. 'Watch out for the tail!' People floundered through the water to catch hold of more blanket.

'Pull!' The cry came in unison.

The whale heaved, tail arching through the air again. Water gushed around us as it landed.

'Pull!' Ian's voice was loud.

'Wait for the waves!'

'Now!'

'And again. Pull!'

The whale was struggling, thrashing his tail wildly. I could feel him moving against the sand. Against us all.

'Wait for the waves! And pull!'

The great body was heaving. Panic surged within him.

'We can do it!' I cried to him. 'We can!'

Another heave. His tail lifted and came down hard on sand and water.

'And pull!'

He was fighting us.

'And again. Pull!'

Fighting against us. The whale's eyes stared wildly into mine. I smelled fear.

'Stop!' I cried. 'We're frightening him! We're hurting him!'

With a sudden great heave, the tail swung high. It came down, hurtling through the air toward Dad. *Whoomp!* He was flung sideways, into the foaming water.

'Dad!' Laura's cry.

'Michael!' Kate screamed and ran to his side.

'I'm all right!' he cried, struggling to stand. Sand and water covered him. 'I'm fine,' he said again, holding them both tightly.

The waves surged, ebbed, and surged again.

Everyone and everything else had suddenly stopped moving.

'We'll have to keep him calm.' Jacob's dad was panting with effort. 'Take it more slowly.'

'Maybe if just one person stood at his head and talked to him ...' It was Toni's voice.

'Let Tess do it,' said Colin abruptly. 'She knows him. She's been talking to him all night.'

'No way!' I took a step backward.

'You understand him the best,' Jacob insisted.

I looked at the whale, lying quietly now, sand and water swirling around him. He was so big. If all of us couldn't move him, what could I do? The whale's dark eyes looked silently back.

'It's not possible,' I said.

'It is! You can do it!' Laura now, the believer in miracles.

Surely the waves were getting lower. The tide was turning. We didn't have time for this. There was movement of someone behind me. I saw Mum start to take a step forward. Then Dad's voice, quiet and calm, whispered only for me.

'You only have to try,' he said. 'Just try.'

There should have been the sound of the sea, of people talking onshore, of the whale's sharp blows of air. All I could hear was silence. Was he still breathing? I took a step forward and turned to face him. The dark eyes flickered and followed.

'Do you remember,' I told him, 'that we promised to help?'

More silence. Water and sand bathing us both.

'You have to help, too, you know.' I put my hand gently against his face. 'We can't do this by ourselves.'

The sounds were starting to come back now. A shuffle of a foot, a muffled cough from behind.

A tiny chirrup from the whale.

'It's just a little way,' I said. 'You want to go back to the sea, don't you?'

The eyes blinked slowly and opened again.

'Come on, then,' I said. 'Just a bit forward. And then we'll all rest again.'

I put my face against his. All night we had stayed together like that.

'We'll be with you,' I whispered. 'We'll hold you until you can swim. Trust us.'

One long wave came swirling up the sand. I felt people tense, felt them pull on the blanket.

And felt a tiny movement of the whale forward.

'Please,' I whispered. 'Trust me.'

A quiver of the tail. A tensing of people. A tiny movement forward.

'They're waiting for you out there.' Was I talking or thinking now? 'The other whales, your family. They're waiting for you to return.'

Another chirrup. Another wave surging. Another tug forward.

'You can do it. It's just a little way.'

A larger wave this time. A larger movement.

'It's not far. Your family is waiting.'

Water. Movement. Muscle. He was so close now, so near.

'You only have to try.'

Near. Near. One move more. Near ...

'You can be free. Free, if you try.'

His great body arched, his tail swept the sand. And suddenly he was slipping, thrashing, sliding forward. And floating into the sea.

Chapter 27

He's rolling again,' Mum said quietly. We were already moving, hands reaching quickly below the water to steady the whale's body. We had been keeping him afloat for hours now, taking it in shifts, chest-deep in the cold water. At first, the whale had been so cramped, we had had to hold him upright and rock him back and forth like a baby. Now he was stronger, able to balance easily, and we let him float half free between us. He faced out to sea and bumped gently against our bodies as the swell rocked him. Sometimes we could feel the sweep of his tail through the water as he tested his strength.

'He's okay now, I think,' said Dad. We straightened up.

None of us could remember when dawn had come. The sun should have been strong enough to warm us by now, but the new day had brought dark cumulous clouds that blocked most of its rays. The wind had picked up, too, making small squalls on the water and white-caps farther out in the bay. It blew against our newly wet arms, making us all shiver.

Onshore, Colin and Jacob and their dads were scooping sand again, filling in the trench.

'Best not let anyone know about the whale,' Jacob's dad had said. 'Even if there's nothing to see, the sightseers will still want to stop and gawk from the cliff top.' None of us had thought of that. We could say a sure goodbye to three hundred plants and our plantation if that happened. Colin and Jacob looked exhausted, but they weren't going to stop shovelling. Far above, I saw Toni give a wave from her position at the top of the path. Her job was to turn back any joggers or early morning walkers collecting driftwood — who might suddenly hurry home with stories of a huge pool on the beach and a whole lot of people, and a whale.

'I'll tell them we've found a container we suspect contains nuclear waste,' she said, grinning. 'That should keep them right away.'

The daylight was growing stronger. How long could we keep people at bay? How long before the whale could find the strength to swim free?

'They're still out there.' Laura was watching the distant sea, one hand shading her eyes, the other hugging her body for warmth. Beyond the swirling breakers at the mouth of the bay, we had sometimes seen the black sweep of dorsal fins circling. 'They're still waiting for him.'

The whale knew it too. He was growing stronger, moving and sweeping against our legs more often. Sometimes he made a tiny clicking call, barely heard above the wind.

'Watch out now!' Waves had tilted the whale. He tried to correct his rocking, turned too far to the other side, and went under. Water swept over his head.

'Help him,' said Mum, and we bent and lifted him up again. A snorting sound, a gurgling, and then he blew a great gush of air and water from his blowhole.

'You ungrateful thing!' said Laura. Most of the water had hit her — even her hair was drenched now. You could hear her teeth start to clatter in time with her shivers.

'Go ashore,' said Kate. 'Get something dry to wear. You're getting too cold.'

'No way,' said Laura. She clamped down

hard on her teeth to quiet them. Mum and Kate exchanged looks, but Kate didn't push it. I guess they were freezing, too, but they weren't going ashore either.

You could sense the whale growing stronger, feel his restlessness. He was pushing against us more urgently, so it was hard to stand upright.

'Steady now,' I told him. I stroked his sides, which gleamed in the water and daylight. He sucked in a great gulp of air, then suddenly gave a flick of his tail and let out a piercing whistle. Laura flinched hard and covered her ears. That sound had hurt.

Colin's dad stopped scooping and walked to the edge of the water.

'Don't let him go yet,' he said. 'It's too soon.'

'He's getting impatient,' Mum said. "We can barely hold him.'

'He'll still be too cramped,' he replied. 'If he rolls in deep water and can't pull himself up, he'll drown.'

'Talk to him, Tess,' said Dad. 'Calm him down.'

I ran my hands over his glistening head and looked into the dark eyes. 'Soon now,' I told him. 'Just wait a little longer.' The whistling sound came again, but softly this time.

'He'll be all right once he reaches the other

whales,' said Dad. He, too, stroked the glistening skin. 'I saw it on TV once.' He frowned, as if trying to remember when. It would have been a long time ago. 'The whales in the pack take turns swimming alongside and supporting him.'

'Pod,' said Kate. 'Whales swim in pods, not packs.' She grinned at him. I'd never heard her correct him before.

'Like a pea,' said Dad. He rubbed the whale's head delightedly. 'You're a bit bigger than a pea, my boy,' he said, laughing.

'Trust an intellectual to know that.' Mum was teasing Kate. She looked down at Kate's sopping wet clothes and face. All Kate's hair had finally escaped from its bun and lay in a tangled mass around her shoulders. 'Although you don't look much like an intellectual at the moment.'

'You think you look like a model?' laughed Kate. She took up a fake catwalk stance, hand on hips, head thrown back. 'And here comes the lovely Margot,' she crooned. 'Dressed in the latest smeared face and sopping jeans look. Patrons, do note the artistically designed straggly wet hair.'

'Didn't you say the grunge look is still in?' I said. Got Mum back at last. 'You've raised it to new heights.'

'New depths, more like it,' said Dad.

The whale was chirruping and clicking, joining in the laughter. There was a quick flick from his tail and a sudden sweep against us, strong and true. Laura staggered and briefly went under, soaked once more.

'You're picking on me,' she scolded him. Her teeth started chattering again.

'Hadn't you better go ashore?' Two tiny lines had appeared on Kate's forehead. Her worry frown was back. 'Please, Laura. You're getting far too cold.'

'I'm fine.' Laura was doing her immovable rock imitation again. Except she was shivering all over.

'Come over here.' Dad reached out. He put both his arms around her body, holding her close, sharing heat. She nestled against him, as if she had done it every day of her life.

Dad looked slowly at me. 'Aren't you cold, too, Tess?' he said.

'No,' I said. He didn't stop looking. 'I'll be all right,' I said. I bent over to check on the whale.

'When I get home,' said Mum, 'I'm going to have the deepest and hottest and longest bath of my life.'

'There won't be any hot water left,' I said, 'after I have the longest shower of my life.'

'But aren't you coming home ... ' began Kate, and suddenly we stopped laughing. 'I'm sorry,' said Kate quietly. 'I just thought you'd be with us.'

I looked at them all. For a while I had forgotten the problems that always lay in wait. It seemed strange somehow that the questions and the decisions were still there. Soon the whale would be strong enough to swim out of the bay and be free. But I would still be trapped.

'I don't mean to hurt you,' I said slowly to Kate. I shot a glance at Dad, tried to smile reassuringly at Laura. 'I really don't know what I want to do yet.' Would my whole life be like this? Always having to decide and trying not to hurt — or be hurt.

'You worry too much,' said Kate. That was a fine one, coming from her! I laughed.

'Let's all start with hot coffee at our place,' said Mum. 'Throw Laura into the bath to thaw her out. And then see how much hot water is left. Maybe that will help you make a decision.'

'I'd kill for a coffee,' said Dad. His voice was really quiet. He was looking at Mum and Kate, checking to make sure he was actually invited too. Mum nodded at him.

'Way too strong and about three spoons of sugar,' she said. 'If I remember.'

Laura slowly leaned forward, away from the warmth of Dad's body, and touched my arm.

'Come home with us,' she said quietly. 'Stay with me.'

'I'm not sure ... ' I said.

'I need you, Tess.' God, she broke my heart.

'You still don't know,' I told her, 'how strong you really are.' She had stood tall and fierce in the parking lot and made the whole family bend to her will. She could get up on a trampoline with hundreds of people watching and never miss a landing. She could float through the air, turning and soaring, almost flying.

'Oh, Tess!' she wailed. 'Please stay!' She leaned closer so that only I could possibly hear her. 'What about the nights?' she whispered. 'The dreams ...'

'Even if I'm not there,' I told her softly, 'you'll still have the dreamcatcher.'

'No.' She shook her head. The whale bumped gently against our legs.

'Take it with you,' I said.

'I can't!' Her voice was a cry of longing and sadness. 'You need it too!'

The whale gave a tiny mew. I stroked his sides slowly.

'I don't.' The words came suddenly. They

surprised us both. 'I don't,' I said again. And this time, somehow, I felt it was true. I leaned forward to touch her wet hair and felt the skin of the whale smooth and strong against me. 'The dreamcatcher is yours.' The words were a gift, a freedom. 'I don't need it anymore.'

Chapter 28

O n the top of the cliff, Toni was waving arms at her third set of people, no doubt expanding on the lies about nuclear waste and toxic barrels. It would probably be all over the front pages of the paper tomorrow. But at least our plants would be safe. Colin and Jacob and their dads had finished filling in the pool and were packing up great armfuls of wet clothing and buckets and blankets. People would be coming onto the beach soon, walking around from the point, scrambling down other paths. Toni wouldn't be able to stop them. Soon they would come. Too soon.

The whale felt it, the growing urgency. He was swirling between us, pushing against our legs and forcing us into deeper water. Laura was up to her chin already, almost out of her depth.

'Don't let him swim out!' called Colin's father. 'He's not ready yet.'

'Gently,' I told our whale. 'Be patient. It's not long now.'

His head butted against me, trying to push through.

'Just a little more time,' I promised. 'Gently now.'

The buffeting was getting stronger, pushing me backwards. I could no longer feel sand beneath my feet.

'We're getting too deep!' cried Dad. He, too, was treading water, his shirt dragging at his arms.

'Come here. Stay here.' Kate was trying to coax the whale.

He surged against us, moving out into deeper water, pushing us aside.

'Not yet!' I cried to him. 'Not yet!' He was swimming close to the surface. Swimming slowly, but I could only just keep up.

'Tess!' Dad called. 'Come back! It's getting too deep.' They had all fallen behind now, struggling back to the shallows and shore. I kept swimming. It was only the whale and me now. My whale.

'Slowly,' I whispered to him. 'I'm with you.' I could hear his tiny chirrup through the water as I swam.

'Tess! Come back!' Whose voice was that? The water was getting rougher now, buffeting against us. The smooth sides of the whale lurched as he turned into the waves. I stopped swimming and rested my hands against his sides until he found balance once more.

I'm here, I told him silently. I didn't need to speak. *You're safe with me.*

Swimming again now, into the waves. Fins slicing the water, arms strong and sure. It was what I had trained for. All those hours, all those days. Swimming and swimming, free with my whale.

I'm with you. I sent the words. *We're safe now.* Another roll, I moved closer to help, but his tail flicked, and he was upright again. We kept on swimming.

Out past the breakers, other fins circled and moved. *They are waiting,* I said. The words drifted through water and mind. I didn't lift my head. Arms moving strong, forever. *Your pod, your friends. They've been waiting all night for us.*

A click, a chirrup. He knew that.

We're nearly there. So close now. I could see the breakers ahead, foaming at the mouth of the bay. The shore was a far distant memory. Spray floated through the air, and there were faint whistling sounds through the water. They were calling us.

He slowed, stopped swimming. One dark eye looked into mine and blinked. Again, the soft whistling sound came, and his mouth opened a fraction in its absurd grin. I ran my hands over his sides, treading water and patting the huge dorsal fin. A sharp, piercing whistle came over the waves. I felt muscles gather, tense — and suddenly he was diving, sounding, plunging through the water. And I was moving with him, pulled by fin and water, surging with him. Down, down, down. Water rushing by us. Down, down, down. We were swimming, we were flying. It was the dream of last night, and my whale was making it come true. Down, down, down.

Abruptly my hands were torn from him. Water churned, twisting, tumbling me in the wake made by the great tail. My lungs burned, wanting air, the old dream was back now. I couldn't breathe, but did I really need to? I couldn't remember. Slowly, I stopped turning. I didn't need to swim. The water was calm and deep below the surface. I drifted.

I saw the sunlight, felt it hurting my eyes as I floated towards it. Then the sound blasted at me, a huge pounding from the breakers as I broke through the water into air. There were more noises, the rush of wind and water, the pain of gasping as I fought for breath. And then the sound of my name carried high into the air.

'Tess! Tess!'

Far from shore, someone was crying and waving, his face almost lost against the surging waves.

He was too far out, it was too dangerous. He should not have been there.

'Tess! Tess!' A cry of fear and want and longing. 'Tess!' My name.

On the far side of the breakers, I saw a whale fin slice through the water, heading out to sea. Another followed and another. The pod was leaving. The whale was swimming free.

'Tess!' The breakers surged, sucking at me. I struggled to breathe, water was churning at my face. 'Come back, Tess!' I knew the voice now.

'Dad!' I cried. I turned and waved, heard his voice call my name once more. I kicked against the waves and started swimming again. The breakers were surging at me, pulling me to them. But my arms were light and strong and free. And I never doubted for a moment that I'd make it home.